HUNTING FOR REDEMPTION

A COLLECTION OF HUNTERS BOOK ONE

TOBY WISE

Hunting for Redemption© 2022 by Toby Wise

All rights reserved. No part of this book may be used or reproduced in any manner whatsoever without written permission except in the case of brief quotations for book reviews.

This book is a work of fiction. Names, characters, businesses, organizations, places, events, and incidents either are the product of the author's imagination or are used fictitiously. Any resemblance to actual persons, living or dead, events, or locales is entirely coincidental.

Book cover by Vicki Brostenianc

Beta Services by Kirk from LesCourt

Formatting by Pumpkin Author Services

JEFF

I WAS SO sure the case was done and closed.

It was so obviously a vampire. He was losing control of himself, draining people in their homes. It was *so* black and white.

"Fuck," I murmur to myself, opening my eyes slowly, wishing my vision would stop being so fucking blurry so I could actually see my surroundings. I was very wrong about this case being done. I try to move my hands and find them cuffed behind the chair I'm sitting in, the metal jingling behind me. The sound is too loud in this otherwise silent room.

My heart picks up speed as I realize the situation I've found myself in. I'm chained to a chair in someone's basement. I look all around but find myself alone. The tiniest bit of relief hits me as I realize the rest of the crew is safe. It's just me here.

When we got to the town, we took our time investigating. There were three bodies, all three had been completely drained of blood, bite marks clearly present and it wasn't hard to realize fangs made these marks. Someone was killing innocent people and based on the evidence, they were slowly losing control. If we didn't stop them now, we knew they would just keep killing.

We did what needed to be done.

It was me who finally found the vampire. He tried to fight back. He tried to drain me as well. But my silver blade was sharpened just that morning. With all my might I took his head clear off his shoulders, stopping him once and for all.

My head throbs with each beat of my heart and my vision is dangerously close to going dark once again. But I fight myself to stay awake and present. I blink over and over until my vision clears enough for me to get my bearings a little better.

Definitely in a basement. There are a few tiny windows at the top of the walls and it appears to be nighttime. Okay, so I haven't been out too long.

What's the last thing I remember? Fuck. I was walking into town by myself. I was planning on hitting the gas station for some marshmallows for Carlos because I forgot to grab them earlier.

I can't believe this is happening. In all my years of being a hunter, I've never been so fucking blindsided before. Well, not since Trish and finding out all the bullshit she was into. My sister turned out to be a rogue hunter, killing supernatural beings just for being different than herself. But since then, I've been so fucking *careful*.

The click of heels against the floor draws my attention and my eyes go to the stairs, watching as a woman steps into the room with me. Her eyes are hard and angry as she looks at me and a chill goes down my spine.

I clench my hands together, schooling my features as best as I can. I know she can probably smell how fucking terrified I am but I won't give her the satisfaction of seeing me scared.

How the fuck did we miss that there were two of them?

"Glad to see you're awake," she says carefully, coming to stand in front of me before squatting down so we're at the same eye level. This vampire is incredibly pretty with long brown hair and piercing eyes but there's something about the curl of her lip that makes her terrifyingly ugly, like she's more than capable of killing innocent people without a second thought. She's beautiful but cold, the worst combination in my experience. Not too much unlike my sister unfortunately.

"I wish I could say the same to you."

"Funny," she says, her voice saying anything but. She's not amused in the slightest. She's not chatty. That doesn't bode well for me. Usually when they're talkative, I can talk them into letting me go or at least distract them enough to get my hands free. Having her full attention on me like this makes my stomach sink.

"You took something very precious to me, human."

"Your hunting grounds?"

"No," she spits out, her lip curling into a snarl, yet her eyes are tortured with anguish. She's angry but she's also *mourning*. Fuck. "You took my mate away from me. I feel so empty without him. I can't eat, I can't sleep. I can barely function without him here and it's all your fault. You *killed* him!"

"He was draining innocent people!"

"I don't *care!*" The vampire slaps me so hard it makes my head spin a little. "You will pay for this," she says, standing up straight and pacing around the room. With her attention away from me, I begin to wiggle my wrists, trying to get some sort of leverage to pull them free or loosen them enough to start slipping out of them. I really don't want to break my thumbs to get out of these but if that's what it'll take, it's what I'll end up doing. Anything to get the fuck out of here.

"How do you plan on making me pay? A life for a life?" Gods, I really hope that's not the plan.

She turns back towards me, her eyes glaring daggers into me. "Something close enough," she murmurs as she straightens up, seeming to come up with an idea. "I want to make you hurt as badly as I hurt."

"I can take pain," I tell her, clenching my jaw. "Is that your plan? To torture me until you feel I've been hurt enough?"

"Something even better," she says, smiling for the first time since entering the room. I swallow thickly. She comes in close, grabbing my chin between her fingers, forcing me to look up at her. I try to turn away but her grip is too strong.

"What then?"

"I think I'll take that which you hold so fucking dearly,

little hunter. I think I shall strip you of your humanity and watch as *you* become *the monster* you apparently hate so much."

It takes a moment for my brain to process but when it does, my entire body locks up with fear. I tried to hide my feelings but now they're broadcast so clearly across my face. "No."

"Oh yes," she says, the delight evident in her voice as she smiles down at me. "You're going to be a vampire by the morning. I think I'll leave your body to reanimate near the ER, that way you'll have a feast right there waiting for you. Let's see how easy it is for *you* to control the bloodlust. Then your crew will have to be the ones to put you down."

"Please no."

"The perfect plan." She smiles down at me, her fangs falling down into place. I try to move away, scooting the chair back as I attempt to fling myself away from her. "Poetic justice really."

"Don't do this. Please. You can go free. Just leave me."

"Your pleas will get you nowhere. My mind is made up." I watch as she bites her own palm, her blood welling up to the surface.

A scream leaves my throat as her fangs dig into my shoulder. My scream is cut short as her hand finds my mouth. I do my best not to swallow but despite my best efforts, it happens. I know the moment it slides down my throat and my fate is sealed.

I close my eyes as my head grows light. Everything begins going black and with the last amount of energy I possess, I throw out a little prayer to whoever will hear it that I have enough control not to hurt anyone when I wake up again. I've never been big on believing in some deity or god out there, but in this moment, I'm not sure I have anything else.

CHAPTER ONE
AXEL

Buzz. Buzz. Buzz.

The noise of my phone buzzing over and over again wakes me up. I rub at my eyes, trying to push away the groggy feeling threatening to pull me back under. I look at my phone, alertness coming to me so quickly it threatens to make my head spin.

"Fuck," I whisper under my breath, sitting up straight and grabbing my phone. Dakota's name flashes across my screen and I quickly click the big green button, answering his call.

"Dakota? Is everything okay?" Dakota is a shifter I'd met a few years ago. He works in the emergency room so I've bumped into him from time to time. Understandable in my line of work.

"Axel. I'm so happy you answered." His voice is stilted and he sounds out of breath. My stomach sinks.

"What's wrong?"

"Nothing," he says carefully. "Well, nothing *yet*."

"What does that mean?"

Dakota lets out a long breath and I'm already standing up and switching from my pajamas to some normal clothes. "Someone's dumped a body here."

"Fuck," I murmur and if I had a beating heart, I know it would be racing right now.

"Yeah. The thing is, his mouth is smeared with blood and I can smell the change happening. When he wakes up, he'll be turned."

"Double fuck." As quickly as I can move, which is pretty fast being a vampire, I change my clothes and head out my front door. I'm already on my way to the hospital before Dakota can finish filling me in.

"Something tells me he was planted here. I know you mentioned blood bags going missing recently. I have a feeling this is somehow related."

"Triple fuck. I don't know how many more fucks I can give you but what the fuck? I really need to get in contact with a hunter or something."

"I don't mean to alarm you further," Dakota says and I just barely keep myself from groaning. There's *more*? "But this man is a hunter."

"Oh for Fate's sake. This is worse than I thought."

"I'm just glad I found him before he woke up. I'm not sure I would have been able to stop a baby vampire who's experiencing blood lust for the first time."

"I'm here," I tell Dakota, slowing my pace to something more human-like and making my way towards the back doors, by the ambulance bay.

Dakota meets me outside and we both hang up our phones. "Did you drive?"

"I--" I rub the back of my neck. "Okay, so I didn't think that far ahead. I just needed to get here as soon as possible and running was faster."

"And how do you plan on bringing this guy back to your house?"

I give Dakota a shrug. "I guess I'll just carry him."

Dakota stares at me for a long moment before his lips are curling up into a small smile. He shakes his head at me, like only a dad could do. "Come on then."

I follow him into the hospital towards the morgue and a shiver goes down my spine. I come here quite frequently. I'm in charge of the local blood bank. Ironic for a vampire, but what better way to make sure the local vampires are fed ethically. I make sure the humans are all taken care of before using any extra for us.

"Here you go," Dakota says, patting the black body bag that's laid out on the table. There's a couple of blood bags in there as well for you both because I'm sure you'll need it when he wakes up."

I carefully scoop him up into my arms. I take a deep breath and freeze. Something about his scent is raising my hackles, forcing my body to tense. I push that aside for now. My first priority is getting him out of here, getting him somewhere *safe*.

"Hey, Axel? Please take special care of this one."

I nod at Dakota. "I promise," I say with a smile before heading through the halls, careful not to be seen. Once outside, I use all of my energy to navigate the streets towards my house as fast as I can. Thankfully at this time, there's barely anyone out and around. I'm able to get this guy back to my house without an issue or incident which I'm thankful for.

Once inside, I lay him down on my couch, making sure he's as comfortable as possible as the transformation continues to happen. It's in that moment that I realize with a start that I have no idea who this guy is. I don't know even know his name.

I run my fingers through my hair before getting to work. I pull the baby vampire free from the body bag, making sure the blood bags are safely on my end table where they won't fall and break. It wouldn't do either of us any good if this guy woke up inside the body bag and freaked out. I need to try to make his waking up as gentle as possible. That'll help with all the heightened sensations he'll be experiencing.

Once the body bag is out of the way, I let my eyes wander over this man. He has dark hair, dark stubble, full lips. His body looks strong and fit, no doubt from being a hunter. But there's something else, something tugging at the back of my head.

I walk away in order to clear my head, making quick work of getting a washcloth. When I come back, he's still not stirring. As carefully as I can be, I wipe the blood away from his throat. Whoever did this left this man a mess. His blood is along the side of his neck and shoulder, his mouth is covered in someone else's blood. I'm no hunter but if I were, I would promise to fuck over whoever did this.

Changing someone like this is unthinkable. It's disgusting and cruel.

A fire burns inside my chest as I clean this man. I'm not a violent person despite being a vampire but there's something about this situation that boils my blood with rage. My fangs drop down and a hiss wells up inside of my throat. But I push it down.

What is that *smell*? It smells so fucking good.

I use the cloth along this man's mouth, cleaning the blood away. Once he's clean, my hand lingers, touching his cheek, just above his stubble. His skin is ice cold. The change is happening. The vampirism is taking. Soon he'll be awake.

I touch my own chest, sitting down on the end table in my living room. Something is compelling me to stay put and watch over this man. I've done this before. I've helped baby vampires get on their feet. But this is the first time I feel so *attached*. The feeling is instantaneous and overwhelming.

There's something about this one that's making me care, making me want to make sure he's safe and happy and taken care of. There's something going on inside my chest that I can't quite explain or understand.

"What is it about you?" I whisper to this unconscious man, letting myself reach out and run my fingers through the man's hair. I pull back, clenching my fist. I need to control myself. He's unconscious for fuck's sake.

There's movement. His fingers, they're twitching. Any time now.

For some reason, I find myself excited with anticipation.

If my heart was beating, I know it would be fluttering about with nerves. Why do I feel like a school boy with his very first crush? What the fuck?

His hand twitches again. I take a deep breath and freeze. His scent, it's changing as the transformation is finishing. He smells so *good*. Fuck. Like lilies swaying on a cool summer day. I breathe the scent in deeply, letting it wash me away for a moment.

Holy shit.

All of the pieces start clicking into place. The feeling in my chest, his scent, my need to protect him. Oh gods.

The man before me finishes his transformation just as the life changing realization hits me full force. He opens his eyes, looking straight at me. My true mate is officially a vampire.

CHAPTER TWO
JEFF

PAIN.

Pain is all I know. My lungs are searing, screaming for air. My chest is too tight. My brain is rearranging itself until I don't even know who I am anymore. My throat is burning like I've swallowed hot coals. I can't do this.

And yet, I know without a doubt that I am completely and utterly still. I'm in the void, drifting featherless while agony becomes all I know.

One moment, I am dying. The next, I am dead.

But death doesn't seem to be the end. I don't understand. I should be nothing. This should be the end of the road. But I know there's more to come.

My senses start to come back to me. The first, being my sense of smell. Something in the room smells downright divine. It's lulling me. There's still chaos going on inside of me but as long as I can focus on that smell, I know I'll be okay. I know I can get through this. The smell reminds me of fresh rain. It makes me wanna sit next to a window and watch as it drips down. It makes me want to sink back into warmth.

The next sense that comes back is touch. I can feel myself on a soft couch. I can feel it beneath me. But I can also feel that I am *cold*. Am I dead after all? Is this a final dream? Why am I so cold if I'm truly still alive?

Next is my sense of taste. Gods, I wish it wouldn't have come back. I just barely keep myself from gagging as the taste of copper fills my mouth. I want to spit it out but keep myself completely still, not really knowing if my body will even cooperate if I ask it to move.

Fuck. What the fuck is going *on*? I know I'm here, present in my body but my body doesn't quite feel like my own. I feel different. I feel stronger somehow. I feel more connected to it while somehow also feeling completely disconnected.

I try to clench my fist and I think it responds. I swallow thickly, realizing with a start that I'm parched. I need something to drink.

Blood.

No. What the fuck? That's disgusting. And yet, the thought of blood makes my mouth start to water. It's what my body is craving. It's what my body *needs*.

Oh gods.

I twitch my hand again and this time it responds the way I want it to. I flex my fingers, making a fist before relaxing again. Okay. I can do this. I'm in control. This is still *my* body.

I'm not breathing. My heart is not beating. Yet I am alive. Fuck. The realization washes over me all at once and my eyes prickle with tears I'm not even sure I have. I force myself to slowly suck in a breath and it feels wrong, my lungs not truly needing it but wanting it anyways just so I can breathe in that beautiful scent surrounding me.

Finally, I open my eyes.

There's a man sitting beside me. He's watching me. My hearing comes back to me and it's heightened. I can hear the buzzing of the fridge, the sounds of someone in the apartment over snoring, the sound of the wind outside. Fuck, it's too much all at once and all I wanna do is shut it off but I can't because this is my fucking life now. I just barely keep myself from covering my ears with my hands, wanting everything to *stop*.

"Hey."

The voice startles me and my body tenses. My eyes snap up to meet this man's. The look he gives me is *soft* and it makes me fucking *ache* in a way I don't understand.

"You're okay," he whispers, trying to soothe me but I don't deserve it. I shake my head and look away, unable to handle the gentleness in his eyes. "You are. Everything is overwhelming right now but it'll be okay. I promise."

I lick my lips, trying to get my mouth to cooperate and talk back. But everything is too dry, too parched. "Thirsty," I just barely get out before I'm choking on nothing, my throat *burning*.

"I've got something for you but I need you to try to drink slowly. I don't want you to choke or get over-whelmed, okay?"

I nod my head in understanding. The man readjusts, his movements slow and calculated. I'm sure he's trying not to spook me. Normally I would scoff at the idea. I'm a hunter for fuck's sake, but right now I feel on edge, ready to bolt at the simplest things.

"Here," he whispers, pulling a bag from behind his back. My body locks up and my eyes focus on the red liquid inside the bag. Fuck. I've never wanted something as much as I want that bag right now.

With speed I didn't even know I was capable of, I grab the bag from his hand, jumping over the back of the couch. I squat down behind it, hiding myself as I tear into the bag with my teeth, sucking the liquid out of it with haste.

Fuck. Holy shit. As the blood finds my mouth, I let out a deep sigh. This is the most delicious thing I've ever drank in my entire life. Perfectly done steak? Ice cream? Hot lava cake? None of those things compare to the taste of this blood. I could just drink and drink and drink forever.

But that's a problem, right?

Why would that be a problem again?

Gods, I can't even remember. All I can do is continue to drink deeply until the bag is completely gone. I throw the bag on the ground with a growl, a sound I didn't even know I could make radiating from the center of my chest. Before I can stand up and demand another bag, a bag is being tossed over the couch for me.

I scramble to grab it, ripping it open in the same fashion as the other, drinking my fill. Fuck, it's so good and I'm not sure I'll ever have enough of it. The compulsion to just keep drinking until I'm satisfied is there. Will it always be like this? Will I always be so fucking out of control? Will I become a monster?

I finish the second bag of blood as the thought crosses my mind and for the first time since waking up, a bit of clarity hits my mind.

I don't want to be a monster. I can't be. I've worked so hard righting wrongs in the supernatural world. What would Dakota think? What would Elwood and Rhett think of me? I've made it my life's mission after stopping my sister to do whatever it takes to gain redemption. How ironic it would be to become one of the monsters I hunt.

I fall onto my ass, my back pressed up against the back of this guy's couch. I close my eyes, covering my face with my hands. I let out a broken noise before sucking in a deep breath, searching for that fresh rain scent that seems to help center me. I find it and latch onto it, letting it sink into my very lungs, holding on so tight hoping it'll ground me.

"I'm a monster," I choke out, my voice coming out cracked. "I'm a fucking monster."

The man is back. I'm not sure when he moved but suddenly he's kneeling before me, his presence soothing me. I'm so thankful I'm not alone right now. I don't even know who he is but he's saving me from myself right now.

"You're not," the man says and I cling to his words. I pull my hands away from my face and stare up at him. "What happened to you wasn't your fault. This is going to be a fucking journey though. But you're going to be okay. Just because you're a vampire, doesn't mean you're a monster."

I didn't want to think the word. I didn't want to believe it. But now it's been confirmed. I am a vampire. That fucking woman stripped my humanity just like she promised. Fuck. I can't do this. I can't fucking do this.

I get my knees under myself before flinging myself forward into this man's arms. It's unfair, to cling to him this way. Thankfully he wraps his arms around me and holds me tight against his chest. That's when I notice he has no heartbeat. He's like me.

He runs his fingers through my hair. "You're okay," he murmurs, "I've got you."

My eyes blink slowly. I'm overwhelmed and exhaustion pulls at me. This has been too much and I'm starting to shut down. My body and my mind need a break and sleep will do that. I sink against this man and let him hold me.

"I'll take care of you. I've got you."

I don't know why, but I trust him. I believe that he has me. I trust that he'll take care of me. I close my eyes and let the darkness take over.

CHAPTER THREE
AXEL

I LEAN against the door frame. Watching someone sleep is probably creepy, right? Yet I can't seem to pull myself away.

The moment he'd fallen into my arms, I was lost. His smell invaded my nose, further cementing what I already knew to be true; this man is my mate. He's the other piece of my soul. He's *here*, in my home, and instead of this moment being one of joy and celebration, it's one of horror. My mate is in pain I can't even imagine.

All I wanna do is go to him and hold him close. But I can't. Not yet anyway.

Right now I just have to be here for him however he needs. I'll make sure he doesn't hurt himself or anyone else. I'll make sure he's fed.

Gods, how do I tell a newly made vampire that not only is his life turned completely upside down but also that he has a true mate? That's way too much for him to handle all at once.

I have to put my own wants aside and make sure he's

okay, that's my main priority right now. Of course I want to take care of him. If he was just some random guy who'd been turned, I would still be here, doing the same thing. But fuck, I'd be lying if I said I'm not fucking *compelled* to help this one even more.

He's my mate.

He's my *mate*.

What a fucking trip. I've been an adult vampire for a couple decades now and I never dreamed of finding my mate *like this*. In my head it would be some sort of meet cute. We'd bump into each other at a coffee shop. Or maybe he'd come into the hospital to donate blood. Or maybe he'd be a shifter I met out on a run. But this? The idea of helping my mate through his transformation as the catalyst for our meeting?

Fuck me running. What a way to bring us together, Lady Fate.

I straighten, noticing the man in my bed beginning to stir. I stay completely still, not wanting to scare him. Everything must be so heightened and overwhelming, I'd hate to accidentally add to that.

"Fuck," comes from the mound of blankets before a head is popping up, hazel eyes meeting mine. I give a soft smile, raising my hand at him. In response, he lets out a long groan, flopping back against the pillows. I can't help but chuckle.

"How're you feeling?"

"Fucking awful," he groans out, his voice less scratchy than it was the first time he woke up. That's an improvement. "I'm so thirsty. But the idea of drinking blood from a bag again makes my stomach turn."

"That's okay, I can take care of that." I turn to walk out of the room but his voice calls out to me, making me pause.

"Wait," he murmurs, his eyes just barely peeking out from beneath the blankets. "What's your name?"

"Axel."

"I'm uh, you can call me Jeff."

Jeff. My mate's name is Jeff. "It's nice to properly meet you."

There's a long pause where he just watches me before he's ducking back under the covers. "You too," he murmurs and I find that to be my cue to step away.

I can't help but smile as I get to work preparing Jeff's next 'meal'. I don't blame him for hating the blood bag. There's something animalistic that takes over when first turned. I've seen my fair share of baby vampires. Some of them tear into bag after bag after bag, their self-control completely gone whenever blood is around. And then there are some like Jeff, who take everything as a challenge of discipline. I wish it didn't have to be like that but I would be lying if I said I wasn't impressed.

No, it's not bias because he's my mate. Not at all.

Hopefully Jeff has a bit of a sweet tooth. I've found this little drink has helped baby vampires at first. I make myself a mug, pouring the majority of it into one of my thermoses, that way it has a top to it so Jeff doesn't have to *see* the blood he's drinking.

"Jeff?" I murmur, stepping into my bedroom once more. Instead of finding my mate tucked under the blankets, he's now sitting up. The blankets are pooled around his waist, leaving his upper body exposed. Sure, he's wearing a tee shirt but still, my stomach flutters at seeing him like this.

If only his shirt wasn't ruined from all that blood.

Jeff looks up, his eyes darting to the mug in my hand. He makes a soft, questioning noise as I step into the room, coming to sit beside his hip on the bed. I hand him the thermos.

"I hope you have a tiny bit of a sweet tooth," I say gently, sipping at my own drink and making a happy noise. "This is one of my favorites."

"What's with the thermos?"

"So you don't have to look at it. Hopefully that helps a little bit. You can just close your eyes and imagine it's a cold night in a cabin somewhere, enjoying a steaming cup of hot cocoa."

Jeff snorts. "Doubt it but it's worth a shot I guess." I watch as he brings his cup to his lips, taking a deep sip. A lot of baby vampires would get one hint of blood and begin guzzling the entire cup. But Jeff takes his time. I can see he wants to chug it, but he holds himself back. Pride wells up inside of me. He's doing so well.

"Do you like it?"

Jeff looks at me, his eyes narrowing. "I can still taste the blood. But it's sweet and chocolatey. I like it." He takes another sip. "Can you do the same thing with coffee?"

I think for a moment. "I've never tried but I don't see why not. We'll try that next."

Being this close has my body reacting. I want to be closer. I want to bury my face against the underside of his throat. I want to bite him and kiss him and lick the blood from his lips. Fuck, I want so much.

But I hold myself back the same way Jeff holds himself back from chugging his blood. Even though everything inside of me is begging me to lean forward and kiss him, that's the last thing he needs right now.

Jeff clears his throat and I look over at him, not even realizing I'd zoned out. He looks almost sheepish as he hands the thermos back. "Thank you."

"No worries. Adding the chocolate is something I learned years ago to help ease people into drinking."

"Not that. Well, yes that but not *just* that." Jeff runs his fingers over his throat, picking some dried blood away. I grab his wrist, gently pulling his hand away. Sparks run down my spine at the simple touch and I can't help but wonder if he's feeling the same thing. Our eyes meet. "Thank you for taking care of me. You certainly don't have to, but I appreciate more than you know. I could have hurt a lot of people if I'd been outside when I woke up."

"I won't let that happen," I tell him softly, needing him to know I'll be here to keep him safe, even if that means keeping him safe from himself. "You're safe here."

He gives me a small nod. "I *feel* safe here. I don't really understand it, but I do."

"That makes me happy to hear," I say, standing up. I can't tell him he feels safe because I'm his true mate, the one destined to help him through thick and thin by Lady Fate herself. Gods, this poor guy just had everything he's ever known change in the blink of an eye. I have to do everything in my power to make this transition as easy as possible and not add to complications.

I nod over towards the other door in my room. "You can have a shower if you're feeling up to it. Might do you some good to get the last of that blood washed away."

"Yeah, that's a good idea." Jeff slowly stands up, not unlike a newly born fawn getting used to their legs. He turns to look at me, opening his mouth like he wants to say something before he's shaking his head and turning towards the bathroom. I watch him as he goes.

Do I already have it bad for this guy? I can't, right? I've only just met him.

And yet, not only do I wanna follow him into the bathroom so I can see what his dick looks like, but I also want to hold him and stroke his hair as he falls asleep. Is this what it's like when you find your true mate? Just an overwhelming bombardment of feelings washing over you? Fuck. I'm so screwed.

CHAPTER FOUR
JEFF

THE WATER FALLS OVER ME, washing away the last of the blood. I've scrubbed my neck near raw, making sure it's all gone. I'm tired of smelling it as it clings to my skin. All I wanna smell is-- I duck my head under the water, trying to get myself to stop thinking about the beautiful man whose shower I'm currently using.

Is this some sort of weird vampire *thing*? Did I accidentally imprint on the first person I saw when I first woke up? Why the fuck do I want to bury my face against his throat and smell him? Why do my fangs itch to bury themselves in his shoulder? Why does my body start to feel *alive* when I'm around him despite knowing I'm *undead*?

There's no denying he's beautiful with his dark hair that curls around his ears and his kind, brown eyes. He's a little smaller than me which makes my stomach flutter with *something* I'm not ready to name. His smile makes my lips curl up in response. He's *gorgeous*. But he's more than just a pretty face, he's also kind.

My stomach swoops in a pleasant way as I think about the chocolate blood he'd given me. It felt like he was being gentle with me, taking care of me. It's been a long time since someone has taken care of me instead of the other way around. I've made it my mission to care for other people. Sure, it's unconventional but taking care of the supernatural and shielding humans away from it is important. I don't regret it in the slightest.

My mind goes to my team and I wince. If my heart was still beating, it would be racing with worry. I need to contact them but I'm not sure I even have my phone anymore. Did that woman steal it? Did she text them and let them know I was dead? Fuck, they must be so worried about me.

I need them to know I'm okay, but I also know I can't go to them. Not yet. Not until I know I won't hurt them.

There's a darkness swirling inside of me. I can feel it. It would be so *easy* to just shut it all off, to lose myself to the blood lust. It wouldn't even hurt, really. But once it's flipped, I don't think I could ever come back. It's not worth it, to even entertain the idea. I shut it down, putting a lid on it and shoving it to the furthest darkest corner of my mind. I will fight to keep my humanity. I won't let this random vampire win.

Letting out a long sigh and dunking my head under the hot water one more time, I turn the water off and step out of the shower. For a moment, my skin is pink from the heat of the shower. For just a moment, I can almost pretend nothing is wrong. But in the next moment, the pink fades, leaving behind the same paleness of before.

able to hear it, or smell it. It's not worth it. Not if I want to keep even a shred of dignity alive.

I might not be alive but my ego is still thriving and I would really like to keep it that way.

Once I've gotten myself under control, I step out into the living room. I let my nose guide me, which is weird as fuck but also kind of cool, to finding Axel. He's sitting at his kitchen table, his phone in his hands. He looks up at me, smiling. I curse my stomach for fluttering like a teenager seeing his crush. That's not what this is. Right?

"Hey," I say, sitting down across from him. "Would it be okay if I used your phone? I think mine was either stolen or left in that basement. I wanna let my team know I'm okay."

"Your team?"

"Yeah." I nod, tapping my fingers against the table. "I'm a hunter. Which is incredibly ironic now, I know that. I have four guys on my team and we work together to stop the supernatural from hurting people."

Axel clears his throat. "I assume you don't hunt for sport?"

"Fuck no," I grit out. I clench my hands against the side of the table, only stopping when I hear the table creak, like it might literally break under my strength. I let go quickly, closing my eyes a moment. Fuck, I need to learn to keep myself in check or I'll be losing control around every corner. "Sorry about that," I say after a moment, opening my eyes again and finding Axel just watching me carefully.

"That's alright. I'm impressed with your self-control if I'm honest."

I snort, shaking my head. "What self-control? I almost

just broke your table because you just happened to blindly stumble onto my past trauma."

"But you didn't actually break it. You think this is my first table, Jeff? It's not. Not by a long shot," he tells me, letting out an amused chuckle.

"You do this often? Bring in newly turned vampires and rehabilitate them?" I ask, wanting to get away from talking about me. Axel's accidentally struck a nerve and I'm doing my best not to let my metaphorical feathers be ruffled.

"My house has somehow become a bit of a wayward halfway house. I help people get back on their feet when the need arises. I've helped raise a few baby vampires in the past." Axel shrugs like it's no big deal. I can feel my heart softening the more I get to know Axel. Not only is he beautiful, but he has a good heart as well.

"That's--" I look away, clearing my throat. "That's really admirable."

"Almost as admirable as a hunter keeping humans safe," he says, smiling at me. Axel slides his phone across the table and I take it gratefully.

"Thank you. I really hope they're not too worried about me. Hopefully they don't fucking hate me."

"If they truly are your team, then there's no reason for them to hate you. They'll probably be relieved to hear that you're safe." I give him a small, somewhat sad smile as I stand up, giving myself the illusion of privacy. "I'm actually going to step out for a moment, so I don't accidentally overhear your conversation, okay? Stay inside for now. I'll just go down to the gas station and then come right back."

"That sounds good. Thank you," I say again, really

needing him to understand how thankful I am for this. For him.

"It's no trouble at all." Axel puts on a jacket and steps out. For the first time since turning, I am completely and utterly alone. I tuck my nose into the front of Axel's hoodie again, letting it soothe my flayed nerves before shakily typing in Ronny's phone number.

CHAPTER FIVE
JEFF

"Hello?"

"Hey," I breathe out, finding that my voice is caught in my throat. The amount of relief I feel from hearing Ronny's voice is unexplainable. "Ronny?"

"Oh my gods," Ronny blurts out, "Jeff? Is that you? Fuck, where are you, bossman? We can be on our way right now."

"No, no," I say right away, a prickling sensation gathering behind my eyes. Fuck. I didn't realize how badly I needed to hear my teams' voices until right now. All of my emotions are heightened, threatening to choke me. I tuck my nose into Axel's hoodie, breathing him in and letting his scent calm me down. "You can't come. But I'm--" I stop myself from saying alive. Because really, that would be a lie. Kinda? Fuck. Why does vampirism have to be so goddamn confusing? "I'm okay," I say instead.

"You don't sound so good," Ronny says, his voice filled with suspicion. Not that I blame him. I would be suspicious if our roles were reversed. "If you're being held against your will, say a sentence with peanut butter in it."

"Ronny," I say slowly, needing him to hear my sincerity. "I'm safe. I'm somewhere safe at the moment being taken care of. I promise you."

"Good enough for me. I have your location based on the cell phone you're using."

"I told you not to come here!"

"But, bossman!"

"No buts, Ronny. It's not safe," I tell him, trying to ignore the way my voice is growing pitchier with worry. I don't know if I can control myself around my team. What if I do something to hurt them? What if I'm driven to bite them? What if the thirst becomes too much. No, I won't put them in harm's way.

"You said you were safe but now you're not in a safe place? Make it make sense, Jeff."

I let out a long sigh, rubbing tiredly at my eyes. "Okay. So here's the thing."

A long moment passes. And then another. When I still don't say anything, Ronny jumps back in. "Go on, Jeff. Spell it out for me."

"Can't you just trust me?"

"I can. And do. Very much so. With *my life* even. But right now you're being suspicious as hell. Maybe you're some sort of shapeshifter who's stolen Jeff's voice and using it as leverage to get me to fall into your trap."

That finally makes me crack the tiniest smile. I've trained my team well and Ronny knows his stuff, even if he goes about it in the cheesiest ways at times.

"Alright. I can prove I'm not a shapeshifter by reminding you of that case we took in Vegas last year--"

"And I think I've heard enough!" I chuckle, fondness making my chest warm. "You're definitely the real Jeff." I hear some shuffling from the other line before someone else is taking the phone.

"Hey, Jeff. It's Cooper. What do you need from us?"

My chest loosens. I knew they would have my back, even if it meant a little bit of interrogation before we got to work. I smile as I sit back in my seat.

"Glad to hear your voice, Cooper."

"Yours too."

"I need a delivery to the address Ronny was tracking me at. But I need you to leave the box at the door."

"Okay," Cooper says, his voice sounding slightly unsure. I hear him ask Ronny about talking to me about a code word and hear Ronny yell about being competent despite being a computer nerd. "What sorta delivery do you need?"

"I would love everything you have about baby vampires. How they're made, how they're fed. Any sort of information you have about the connection sires have on the vampires they create. Just anything like that."

There's a long pause that makes my stomach sink. I wait for disapproval or hate or disgust.

"Oh, Jeff."

I push my fingers against my closed eyes so hard I begin to see spots, trying to fight against the onslaught of emotion barreling through me. I let out a shaky breath.

"Umm, yeah," is all I can find to say.

"You're okay, Jeff. We've got you. Okay?"

A noise leaves my lips, something between relief and a sob. It gets stuck in my throat. "Are you?" Upset? Disgusted? Ready to come put me down?

"It doesn't matter," Cooper says, his voice leaving no room for argument. "And even if we were upset, you shouldn't care. All that matters is that you're *safe*. Are you still you?"

I take a moment to answer, really feeling searching within myself. I'm still Jeff. I'm still a hunter. I still love my team. I still want to do my best to do *good*. "Yes."

"Exactly. Hold onto that, Jeff."

I stare at Axel's tablecloth for a long moment. Finally, I find the words I'm looking for. *"Thank you."*

"You've no reason to thank me. You'd do the same if this was reversed."

I shake my head even though I know Cooper can't see it. "But still. Thank you."

Instead of adding more, Cooper pivots topics back to the matters at hand. "I'll have that package on your doorstep by the end of the night. Do you need anything else? Clothes? Weapons?"

"Some of my own clothes would be nice." *I guess*, I add in my head. My fingers play with the front of Axel's hoodie. Sure, my own clothes would be comfortable but Axel's feel so much better and smell so good.

Why does his scent make me feel so at home?

"You got it, boss. Now hunker down and take care of yourself, alright? We've got the rest covered."

Once the call is over, I stand up. All of the adrenaline of

making that call comes crashing down and I find myself wanting to go for a run. Or shoot something. Or do a thousand push-ups. Or drink an entire deer dry.

Wait. Fuck. No. Not that one.

I shake out my hands, getting them to stop shaking as I step out of Axel's kitchen towards his bedroom. I'm not sure what compels me to find my way into his bed once again. Maybe it's the fact that it smells so much like him here, or maybe it's just the idea of laying down and sleeping this adrenaline haze off. Either way, I find myself face planting into Axel's bed.

That was a mistake.

The moment my face hits his pillow, I'm lost. His scent surrounds me, setting something buried deep inside of me ablaze. One moment, I'm thinking of taking a nap and the next, I'm rock hard in my sweatpants, just barely keeping myself from humping Axel's sheets.

Gods, what's coming over me?

I flip over onto my back, staring down at my erection which is tenting the front of my pants. I close my eyes, listening for any signs of Axel's return. When I come up empty, I throw the final shreds of my self-control right out the window.

My body is burning with lust so bright I'm not sure anything will be able to put it out until I've found some form of relief. Fuck. Why is my body reacting like this? Why do I crave Axel so fucking badly? Is this part of becoming a vampire or is this something else entirely?

I run my hand down my chest towards my cock. The breath I don't even need to survive stutters in my chest.

Fuck. Everything feels so good, so overwhelming. Like a fan stirring the flames, my lust is only growing hotter.

The moment I wrap my hand around my aching cock through my sweats, I know there's no turning back. There's no way I could pull myself away from the edge. It's too late, I'm already gone.

"Fuck," I gasp out, throwing caution to the wind and instead, pushing my hand into my pants in order to stroke myself properly. "Fuck, yes."

The only thing that would make this better is if Axel was here with me.

I shouldn't be thinking about him like this. I shouldn't be touching myself *in his bed,* while wearing his clothes. But I can't seem to stop myself now that I've started. I've opened the door a crack and now the floodgates of feelings are rushing towards me and I have nowhere to run.

Precum makes the slide easy as I stroke my cock, tightening my fist around the head. So many things about myself have changed in such a short period of time but I'm happy to report that *this* seems to still be the same.

I tuck my nose into Axel's hoodie and close my eyes, letting his scent wash over me. This feels so wrong and yet, there's something about it being wrong that seems to make it even hotter. I'm going to mark his sheets with my cum.

A growl rips through my chest without my permission at the idea of marking Axel's bed in my scent. Fuck. Some animalistic part of me needs it more than I need anything else. I want him covered in my cum, in my bites, in my marks. I want my team to show up and see him completely claimed by me.

Where are these thoughts coming from? And why don't I want to push them aside?

"Fuck! Axel!"

My stomach swoops as his name leaves my lips. Would he like that? Would he beg for my fangs?

My hand moves even faster as I chase my pleasure. It only takes the picture of my fangs plunging into Axel's pale skin to have my orgasm rushing through me. My back bows off the bed as I'm overcome with pleasure. Cum covers the inside of Axel's sweats and that only seems to drive my pleasure higher, knowing his clothes will smell like *me* now. Like us.

As I lay there panting for breath I don't need, my ears pick up a sound.

I completely freeze, looking over at the entrance of Axel's room to find the vampire of my fantasies there. His eyes are wide as he stares at me.

I let out a long sigh and cover my face with my hands. "Fuck."

CHAPTER SIX
AXEL

HOPEFULLY ENOUGH TIME HAS PASSED. I nervously hold the candy I've bought from the gas station in my hand, picking at the corner of it as I walk. I wanted to give Jeff enough time to make his phone call in peace but not leave him so long he'd be tempted to do something stupid, like leave.

As I walk up to my apartment, I do my best not to listen in, just in case he's still on the phone. I don't want to overhear anything he might be saying to his team. Being in the same house as a vampire means little to no privacy which can be jarring for a new vampire.

I run my fingers through my hair. I just want Jeff to transition into his new life as easily as possible. I want the best for him, and it's eating me up inside not telling him the truth about us.

Lady Fate, why'd you have to make this all so complicated for me?

After unlocking the door, I step inside my apartment and freeze. *Oh.* Oh my gods. I take in a deep breath, my body turning into putty at the scent invading my nose. Those lilies are back full force but this time there's another hint to it. Something sweet and earthy. Something that pulls at my instincts that I've kept buried deep inside for a long time. Something that makes my fangs tingle and my cock plump up.

I hear a moan coming from somewhere inside the house. If I was capable of blushing, I know my cheeks would be bright red right now. Should I just turn around and leave? Should I let Jeff finish and pretend this never happened?

I drop the candy when I hear my name. Fuck. *He's calling my name.*

That tether between us tightens. It has a grip around my throat like a leash, tugging me towards Jeff and without my permission, my feet begin to bring me towards my bedroom.

The sounds coming from my room are downright sinful. Moans and gasps and *my name.* Gods, I want to be in there with him. I want to see what he looks like when he's experiencing pleasure. I want to see him completely bare for me, offering his shoulder for my teeth.

Like a moth towards a flame, I find myself in my bedroom door.

I watch with rapt attention as Jeff touches himself, his hand moving beneath his sweatpants that he's wearing. *My sweatpants.* Fuck, he's beautiful. I could get completely drunk off the scent radiating from my bed. His lust is mixing with my scent to create something I don't think I'll ever get enough of.

When Jeff comes, I barely keep myself from following

after him despite not even touching myself. The sight of him like this, experiencing pleasure while no doubt thinking about me is too much. My fingers grip the doorframe, just barely keeping myself from crushing it under my fingertips. I make the smallest noise and suddenly, his hazel eyes are on me.

Jeff's body locks up and his eyes widen. Oh no. I've ruined everything. I've fucked it all up. Fuck.

"Fuck."

Gods, his voice is so breathless. So fucked out. My entire body is tense, prepared to pounce and I just barely keep myself from moving. My instincts are screaming at me full force, begging me to step forward, to claim my true mate. I feel like I'm just barely keeping it together.

"Fuck," Jeff says again, covering his face with his hands.

He looks upset. I hate that he's upset. I hate that I had a hand at making him feel this way.

Without my permission, my feet are moving towards him, stepping over to the bed. I gingerly sit down on the side of my bed. Fuck, he's just come while lying in *my bed*. I shake the thought away, ignoring the way my cock is rock hard in my jeans.

"Hey," I say gently. "It's okay."

"It's not. I'm embarrassed that you've caught me like this."

I shake my head, my hand clenching around nothing to keep myself from reaching out further and touching Jeff. I think if I touch him I won't have the strength to pull away. "Your instincts are heightened to the max right now. Everything feels different."

"It feels different, but some things feel *good*," Jeff says softly, his eyes raising to meet my own.

I'm drawn to him in a way I've never experienced before, like two magnets sliding across a flat surface towards each other. One moment I'm sitting beside him and the next I'm leaning towards him, the same way he's leaning in towards me.

My eyes close as Jeff's lips touch mine, just barely. It's the briefest touch, but it's enough to completely rearrange my world. There's no turning back for me. Jeff is my true mate, and now that I know what his lips feel like, I won't ever be able to kiss another pair. I'll never be able to close this door. Gods, I really need to find the words to explain to him that I'm his true mate. I need to figure out how to explain the idea of true mates to him.

Will he hate me once he knows I was hiding this from him?

Fuck, I'm doing the thing I promised I wouldn't do. I'm taking advantage of him. I'm fucking with him before he's gotten used to everything this new life entails. Time. He needs time.

With every ounce of strength I can pull together, I break away from the kiss. Jeff makes a wounded noise, one I can *feel* inside my chest. My fingers grip the sheets so tight I'm positive there will be holes in them later.

"I'm sorry," I whisper, just barely choking the words out. "I'm so sorry. I shouldn't have done that."

"No, it was me--"

I cut him off, shaking my head. "I'm the one who should be in control. I shouldn't be taking advantage of you while you're figuring all of this out. I'm--" I make a frustrated noise. "I'm sorry, Jeff. I should go and give you some space," I blurt out before standing up and rushing out of the room.

I hear Jeff call my name but I don't stop until I'm back outside, breathing in fresh air that's completely void of Jeff's delicious scent. My head slowly clears and I groan. I'm so frustrated with myself. I thought I had self-control! I thought I could handle this. But apparently having a true mate is like nothing I could have prepared for.

I just hope I haven't hurt Jeff so much that he can't forgive me.

CHAPTER SEVEN

JEFF

I PACE.

As I walk back and forth around Axel's living room, the moment we'd shared plays over and over in my head. I'd kissed him. I'd kissed Axel right on the lips. And he didn't seem to mind it at first. He seemed to enjoy it.

Fuck, his lips had felt so good against my own. They'd felt like they were exactly where they should be. And then he *pulled away*.

Axel had kissed me and then immediately regretted it.

I've had bad dates. I've had my fair share of shitty hook ups. I'm no stranger to rejection. So why the fuck does this one hurt *so badly*? Why does it feel like my unbeating heart is being literally ripped from my chest? Why can't I stop thinking about that kiss?

I rub tiredly at my eyes, trying to shake this feeling. What the fuck is happening? Is this a vampire thing? Will every emotion feel like I can barely swallow them down?

Will everything from here on out be pain and guilt and *overwhelming*?

There's a knock at the door and I spin around, my eyes finding the door. Without my permission, my fangs drop and there's a barely there hiss leaving my lips. I take a deep breath and my body locks up. I know that smell. I *know* that scent.

I rush to the door in the blink of an eye, just barely keeping myself from ripping the door open. I look through the peephole, my chest loosening with relief as I see Cooper there.

"I told you to just leave the supplies at the door."

"I know what you said but I wanted to see you."

"I cannot open this door, Cooper. I can't. I don't want to accidentally hurt you."

Cooper sets down a large box, crossing his arms over his chest. "You're really worried about hurting me? Fuck, Jeff. I know you'd never hurt me. Never."

"I wanna believe that. I really do. But I can't guarantee that."

"Because you're a vampire."

It's not a question. I lean my forehead against the door. Fuck. How did this all get so fucking jumbled up? How did everything get so complicated? I used to fight evil. And now I'm a monster.

"Yes," I tell him, the word coming out in a choked gasp. "Yeah, Cooper. I'm a vampire."

There's a long pause where everything goes still before Cooper is clearing his throat. I look through the peephole again, preparing myself to see a sneer of disgust but instead I find a look of understanding.

"I'm glad you're okay, Jeff. Truly. We'll get through this, okay? We're a *family*. We stick together and we fight not only side by side but also for each other."

I swallow around the lump in my throat, pushing back tears. Can I even cry anymore? Does my body still produce tears? I have no idea and that uncertainty brings a broken sob rushing out of my throat.

"Thank you," I grit out through clenched teeth. "I love you guys. Please make sure the team is up to speed and *please* stay on the lookout and don't go *anywhere* alone. The vampire who did this to me is still at large."

Cooper nods his head, gently touching the door. He can't see me but I still place my hand on the door the same way. I love my team. I love that they're the family who's chosen me the same way I picked them. With them behind me, I know I can do this, I know I can learn to tame the hunger and learn self-control. Their strength leads me on.

"We'll stay on this hunt until it's taken care of," Cooper promises me. "Take care of yourself, bossman. We need our leader, alright?"

"I promise," I tell him seriously.

I wait until I can no longer smell Cooper before I open the door and grab the box he's left me. I bring it into Axel's room, closing the door behind me. No, I'm absolutely not hiding from him. Nope. Not at all. I just want to give him his space for when he gets back home. That's all.

I continue to lie to myself as I open up the box, finding a

pile of old looking books. I pick them up carefully, handling them with the care Cooper would expect. These are precious to him and therefore, they're precious to me as well.

I notice he has some things flagged with little sticky notes so I carefully flip through those pages first. The first page talks about the very first vampire created. Apparently vampirism was initially a curse brought on by a powerful goddess who was jilted by a man. He cheated on her and in return, she cursed him with the need for drinking blood. Later on, Lady Fate looked upon the vampire and decided to show him mercy. She gifted him with the ability to live forever and sire a family through transforming people, or through birth.

I'm fascinated as I read over the words, almost forgetting that this is relevant to my life now. I read about the bond a vampire has with their sire. A freshly turned vampire often feels attached to their creator. Lady Fate wanted this bond to be something special, like a pair of best friends sharing eternity together. I clench my fist, thinking about the way the woman who did this to me took something initially beautiful and corrupted it so thoroughly. That fucking asshole.

I flip through the pages, finding the next tag that Cooper has left me. I read the words 'true mate' and my stomach flips. What's this?

My eyes scan the page, devouring the words before me. Another gift from Lady Fate. She looked at her supernatural children and felt the way they longed to not be alone. She intervened and began to intertwine their soul lines. Every supernatural creature has a true mate out there, the one who would complete their soul.

True mates are drawn together. A tether ties them together, pulling tighter and tighter until they're falling into each other's laps one way or another, destined to find true love once they're together.

I bite my bottom lip so hard it draws blood.

Is that what I'm feeling? Is Axel my *true mate*? But why wouldn't he say something? Why wouldn't he just *tell me*?

I put on my hunter hat, trying to look at this logically.

Axel took me in when I was at my most vulnerable, promising to help me with my transition into the supernatural world. I'm sure he didn't want me to feel like he was forcing himself on me. He was trying to protect me.

My stomach is fluttering with butterflies as I sit back against Axel's sheets, letting this new information truly sink in. Axel is my true mate.

Even as I think the words, they sing with truth inside of me. He's my true mate. That's why he smells so good, that's why I feel so at home here in his space. This is why I feel so fucking *drawn* to him, which is a relief because I was worried I would always feel so fucking overwhelmed for the rest of my undead life but it turns out it's because I'm around my true mate.

A started chuckle escapes me as relief hits me full force. I'm not out of control, I'm just meeting *my mate*.

I continue to read everything that Cooper has left me, wanting as much information as possible. I get so lost in reading that I don't register Axel's arrival until he's knocking on the bedroom door. I startle for a moment before relaxing, setting my book down on the bed.

"Come in."

Axel walks in, looking all matters of shy. After tucking his hair behind his ear, he nervously rubs at the back of his neck. "Hey," he says, his shoulders so tense they're practically touching his ears. I really shouldn't find this so endearing. All of these feelings welling up inside of me finally make sense and I can't stop myself from smiling. "I just wanted to apologize about earlier."

I shake my head. "You have nothing to apologize for," I tell him seriously.

"No, I really do. I shouldn't have let things get so out of hand. You're still learning how to be in this body. I shouldn't add complications to that, Jeff."

"You know what?" I ask, cutting him off and standing up. "I changed my mind. You have one thing to apologize for."

Axel's eyes widen and he stands up a little straighter, hanging on my every word. Good. I want his full attention.

"Anything," he says.

"You can say you're sorry for not telling me sooner." I take another step towards him until I'm right in his space, almost nose to nose.

"Tell you what?"

"That you're my true mate," I say right before I'm kissing him and this time, Axel doesn't pull away.

CHAPTER EIGHT
AXEL

Fuck. Fuck, he knows. How does he know?

I can't focus on working through this logically, all I can do is be washed away in this kiss. Jeff kisses me with a passion I'm not prepared for. It's like nothing I've experienced before. My hands grip the front of his shirt and I'm not sure if I want to push him away so we can talk this out or hold him tight so he can never go.

Thankfully, the decision is taken away from me. Jeff pulls back, resting his forehead against mine. Having him this close is everything I've been craving since he woke up. Was that truly just yesterday? Has it only been a day of knowing this man? How can my feelings be *so* deep already?

"Axel," he breathes, his lips just barely out of reach of my own. "I know you're my true mate."

"How?"

I can feel his smile. "Cooper brought me some really interesting reading material. He's a true keeper of lore and knew exactly what grimoires to bring me. There was an entire section about true mates."

"Oh," I say, my stomach flooding with a mixture of joy and trepidation. I pull back so I can look into his brown eyes. "Are you mad at me? For not telling you?"

Jeff shakes his head, his eyes going soft. "I understand why you didn't say anything sooner. You were hoping to protect me while I was undergoing my transformation. You were trying to do what you thought was right." He leans down and places the gentlest kiss against my lips. "I'm not upset, but maybe next time something like this happens, we talk it out instead, okay?"

There are butterflies zipping around inside my belly at the idea of next time. This sentence implies that Jeff plans on sticking around. He plans on this being a real relationship. I smile so wide my cheeks hurt. "I can handle that," I tell him before pulling him into another kiss.

This kiss feels different. It feels full of potential. It feels like the start to something new, something beautiful. When Jeff's lips part, I push my tongue into his mouth, moaning when our tongues touch for the first time. Fuck, Jeff tastes even better than he smells. My head feels like I'm underwater and the only thing giving me air is Jeff.

Jeff's hand slides under my shirt and a shiver runs through me. "Can I?"

I nod my head, pulling back so that Jeff can easily pull my shirt over my head. His hands slide over my exposed skin, his touches almost reverent in nature. I feel so desired, so fucking *wanted*.

"Fuck," Jeff murmurs, his eyes looking over my chest. "Fuck. You're so hot."

If I was capable of blushing, I know my face would be bright red right now. Instead, I bite my bottom lip, letting his compliment wash over me. "Let me see you," I say, grabbing at his shirt.

Jeff is quickly pulling his clothes off until he's in nothing but his boxers. His body is strong and toned, beautifully pale. There are scars leftover on his skin from being a hunter. He's breathtaking and I thank Lady Fate for giving me such a beautiful mate.

"I have all these instincts that I'm not used to," Jeff murmurs, stepping into my space and running his hands over my sides.

"Like what?"

"I want to bite you so fucking bad. Not to drink from you. I just want to mark you. Is that normal?"

"Very much so," I tell him, desire rushing through me at the thought of having Jeff's mouth on me, leaving marks for me to find before they heal. I want that so fucking badly and I want to do the same to him. "I want to mark you too. I want to claim you. I want to cement our mating." I clear my throat, getting ahead of myself. "But that's only when you're ready. I can be patient, Jeff. I can wait until you're more used to the idea, until you're more acclimated to being a vampire."

Jeff's eyes narrow. "Fuck that, Axel. I want you right now. Can I have you? Please?"

I suck in a shaky breath and nod my head. This is everything I've wanted to hear since Jeff woke up. "Gods, yes."

A growl radiates from Jeff's chest and the noise makes my knees go weak. Thankfully, he's right there to catch me, scooping me up and tossing me onto the bed. A giggle escapes my lips without my permission as I scoot back onto the bed until my head is against my pillow. I shimmy out of my boxers, tossing them onto the floor and spreading my legs for Jeff. His eyes take all of me in and I can *see* his desire for me reflected in his pretty hazel eyes.

"Get over here, my mate."

Jeff pulls his own boxers down and I get to see his hard cock in all its glory. It's a gorgeous cock, hard and long. I can't wait to feel it inside of me. I can't wait to touch it and taste it. I can't wait to both feel pleasure from it and give Jeff pleasure through it.

I reach out my hands, pulling Jeff down against my chest as he crawls onto the bed. Feeling his naked skin against my own makes a noise of pleasure leave my lips. Oh gods. This is amazing yet my stomach blazes, begging for more, begging to feel him stretching me open.

Jeff rides his hips down against me and I tilt my head back, letting out a gasp. "Fuck," I murmur, my skin feeling like it's on fire every place we touch. "Fuck, Jeff!"

"Does it always feel like this? It's overwhelming," he whispers, his mouth going to my exposed throat and leaving barely there kisses.

"No," I say softly, wanting him to understand. "It's *never* felt like this. What we have is special."

Jeff pulls back so he can look down at me, giving me a soft smile. "Good." He runs his nose over mine and I can't stop smiling at such a soft gesture from such a tough man.

"You're special to me too. I know this is all going so fucking fast but this feels like nothing I've felt before. As a hunter I have to trust my gut a lot of the time and right now all my gut is telling me is that this is how things are supposed to go."

I nod, running my fingers over Jeff's sides. "My instincts are saying the same. But I supposed that's how true mates are. They run head first into each other, knowing the other will catch them."

And just like that, we're kissing once more. This time the atmosphere is obvious. I spread my legs further, raising my ass off the bed to thrust against Jeff. Everything inside me is screaming for Jeff to get the fuck inside me.

I quickly nod to my bedside drawer. "Jeff. Get the lube. Please, I wanna feel you inside me."

With lightning fast speed that makes me chuckle, Jeff is diving into my drawer and pulling out the lube. He hands it to me. "Here," he murmurs, "I don't trust myself yet. Can you open yourself up for me?"

I take the lube from him, covering my fingers with it. Jeff shuffles until he's lying on his side next to me, his mouth never leaving my skin. His hand skims up and down my belly, touching me in a way that keeps my excitement high but also relaxes me. He's perfect.

"That's it," he whispers into my ear, making me shiver. I reach down and touch my hole, running my fingers over it and making sure it's nice and slick before pushing the first finger inside myself. I moan at the perfect stretch. "You're doing amazing. So perfect. I can't wait to feel you around my cock, Axel."

Jeff's praise washes over me as I pump my finger in and out, getting used to the feeling before pushing in a second. Jeff's mouth touches my cheek, then my chin, then the side of my neck. His teeth run over my skin in a teasing way and I moan, my skin breaking out with goosebumps at the feeling. Soon those same teeth will be sharp and breaking through my skin to mark me forever as his. The thought has my cock *throbbing* with want. I want that so bad. I fucking *need* it.

"Jeff," I hiss out, pushing a third finger into my hole, making sure I'm nice and ready for his cock. "Jeff, please. I need you."

"You have me," he tells me, his voice dripping with seriousness. "You have me, Axel. I promise."

"Need you *inside me*," I say with a smirk. "Now Jeff! Come on!"

Jeff snorts in amusement, kissing my cheek one more time before turning to lay flat on his back. Instead of getting on top of me, a startled noise escapes me as he flips me over so that I'm straddling his lap. "There we go," he says with a wide smile. "Ride me, Axel."

"Gladly," I say, covering his cock with lube before positioning it at my entrance. I take a steading breath before sinking down. "Fuck," I gasp out as I'm stretched open. His cock feels so fucking good, the perfect width to stretch me and the perfect length to fill me. When I'm sat completely in his lap, I open my eyes, finding his staring up at me in something mixed with awe and lust.

"Jesus," he grits out through clenched teeth. "You feel fucking amazing. Fuck, Axel."

I nod my head. "You do too. So good."

Jeff's hands slide up my spine before they find my head, tugging me down into a brutal kiss. As our tongues collide, I begin to properly ride him, pulling up before slamming back down, fucking myself on his cock. My pleasure is rising higher and higher with every movement and I honestly don't know how long I can keep this up before I'm coming. Fuck, it just feels so good, feels so surreal to be connected to my *true mate* like this.

Something stings my lip and I pull back, seeing blood on Jeff's mouth. His fangs are down and gods, I should find that so fucking *hot*.

"I'm so sorry," he starts to say but I cut him off by leaning down and biting his lip right back.

"Don't be," I tell him with a smile. "Feels good. You look sexy with your fangs down."

"I do?"

"Very much so." Then I smile wide, showing off my own fangs right back. I lick across my sharp tooth, watching as his eyes darken even further.

Jeff grabs hold of my hips, holding me still as he fucks up into me with long, hard strokes. Gods, I love that he's letting himself go, letting himself fuck the way his instincts want him to. Fuck, this feels so good.

"Fuck, Jeff! I'm gonna come! You're gonna make me come!"

"Yes," he hisses out, his voice even deeper than before. "Come for me, Axel. Show me how good I make you feel. Mark me with your cum."

Instinct begins to take over. My fangs fucking *itch* with

the desire to bite Jeff. To mark him as my own. To tie our souls together. I don't fight it.

"Fuck!" I bite down on the meat of Jeff's shoulder, really digging my teeth in good. The taste of his blood hits my tongue and I'm gone. I see fucking stars. My cock throbs as I jolt with pleasure, cum splattering between our bellies and mixing with the already downright divine scent filling the room. I come and I come and I come. I feel like it goes on forever before I'm finally able to have a coherent thought. I gently pull my fangs free of Jeff's skin, looking down at my handiwork with pride.

"Can I bite you?" Jeff asks, his voice sounding strained. "Please, Axel? Please, I want it so bad. *Fuck.*"

"Yes," I say, leaning down to put myself closer to his mouth. He bites down into my skin and I'm lost for a second time. I can feel his cock unload inside my ass and I clench down, wanting it all inside of me, wanting him marking not only my skin but also my insides.

Jeff whimpers and whines as he comes. The feeling of his teeth in my skin is perfect and after a moment, I can feel our bond click into place. He is mine and I am his. We're bonded. We're *mates*.

As Jeff pulls his teeth free, he gently licks the bite, cleaning the small amount of blood away. Then he lays the gentlest kiss against the bite.

"That was," he starts to say but his words cut off, like he's not sure what words to even use.

"It really was," I say back, smiling down at him. "You're my mate now, Jeff. The bites we exchanged won't heal. They've sealed our bond."

His hands hold onto my hips, making little patterns with his thumbs. "Mates," he says slowly, processing this news. When he looks up at me, there's a soft smile on his lips. "I like the sound of that."

I lean down and kiss his lips, both of us smiling into the kiss. I gently pull my hips away from his softening cock, rearranging to lay myself against his chest. He kisses the top of my head, holding me tight.

This is the start of a brand new chapter, one that I'm excited to see through. My only worry is that Jeff is a hunter. Will I fit into that life with him or will he want to return to hunting and leave me behind?

I let out a long breath. That's a worry for another day, I suppose. Right now, I'm going to enjoy the afterglow of being so thoroughly fucked by my true mate.

CHAPTER NINE
JEFF

I TAKE a small sip from my cup before setting it down. I'm trying not to chug the entire glass all at once. This is progress. I feel like my self-control gets better with each passing day.

I need that self-control today more than ever. My crew is coming today. Axel will be here the entire time, lending me strength and making sure I don't hurt them but I would be lying if I said I wasn't nervous as fuck. Even with every precaution in place, I'm still worried I could hurt them. I don't think I'd ever be able to forgive myself if something happened to them because of me.

A hand runs through my hair and I look up, finding my mate staring down at me with a soft smile. Fuck. *My mate.* Who would have thought that being turned into a vampire would give me something as precious as a mate? How lucky am I that the man taking care of me turns out to be just that? Lady Fate really knew what she was doing when she crossed our paths.

I'm so thankful for Axel. He's taken care of me at my most vulnerable. He's been patient with me as I learn to control myself and learn how to interact in this new body. He's been kind and supportive. It was his idea to bring the guys here today because he thinks I'm ready. He's so sure I won't hurt them.

I hope his faith isn't misplaced.

"How are you feeling?"

I grab his wrist, pulling his hand down so I can nuzzle it. "I'm okay. Mostly just nervous."

"How hungry are you?"

"Not too bad," I tell him seriously. "I think I'll be full after this glass."

"Good. Then the temptation won't even be there. Trust me. Once you smell them and they smell like *family* they'll smell a lot less like *food*."

I let out a long sigh. "If you say so."

"I do. Trust me. I've been a vampire much longer than you."

I smile, tugging Axel down so he's sitting in my lap. I run my thumb over his cheek, just looking at how pretty my mate is. "How long *have* you been a vampire?"

"My entire life," he says with a small smile, knowing that's not at all what I meant. But it *is* interesting. I hadn't realized Axel was a born vampire rather than a turned one like me.

"And how old are you, mate of mine?"

"I turn sixty-nine next month."

I smirk plays across my lips. "Well, let me tell you, I

have a few ideas on how to properly celebrate said birthday."

Axel lets out the most adorable giggle, smacking my chest playfully. He shakes his head before ducking down and stealing a kiss. Just then, there's a knock on the door. I swallow thickly, my entire body locking up.

"Hey," Axel whispers, running his fingers through my hair once more. "You're gonna do amazing, Jeff. You can do this."

"I can do this," I repeat, nodding my head. "Thank you for being here."

"There's nowhere else I'd rather be." He picks up my mug of warm blood, handing it over to me. "Finish this and then I'll let them in, okay?"

I silently pick up the mug, drinking the rest of it. The blood is delicious as it slides down my throat and warms me from the inside. I can understand why some vampires become addicted to drinking so much at once. I feel almost *human* when I've just finished drinking my fill. It makes me feel *warm* again. It's an addicting feeling but one I'd rather not chase, not when it could put someone's life at risk. Not when it could make me a monster.

I can hear the door click open from here. I listen closely, able to pick out four sets of footsteps besides Axel's. The tiniest smile plays at my lips. I'm not getting rusty, if anything, becoming a vampire has helped me with things like this. Maybe I'll be able to become an even better hunter.

"Are you sure it's okay that we're here?" Carlos asks. "If it's too soon we can totally wait."

"No, no," Axel reassures them, my stomach warming at

the amount of faith my mate has in me. "He's ready. And I'll be right here to help ground him just in case. He won't admit it but he's missed you all."

"Awww," Ronny coos and I roll my eyes. "Bossman missed us!"

"Of course I did," I say as they come into the kitchen. The first one through the door is Cooper and he pauses for just a moment before smiling and coming to sit down at the table with me. Everyone else follows behind. Martin squeezes my shoulder as he passes me and his scent fills my nose. Axel was right. They don't smell like food, they smell like my *family*. Their scents comfort me.

I can hear each of their hearts beating, the sound throbbing inside my skull. I can imagine the blood flowing through them. But instead of the desire to bite them, I'm overcome with the instinct to *protect them*, to keep that blood flowing at all costs.

I relax back in my chair, looking around at everyone as they in turn, look back at me. I can tell they're assessing me, trying to figure out if anything's changed.

"So," I start, leaning my elbows on the table. A gentle hand touches my shoulder and the smell of fresh rain hits my nose. I smile as I look at my team. "Tell me what we've got on this vampire."

There's a pause before everyone is sinking back into their usual roles. "So I found footage of when she took you. I've got what she looks like. We were also able to find the house she was holding you in, but she hasn't been back since," Ronny, our tech guy, tells me. Something close to pain rings through my chest at the thought of my team seeing that basement, seeing all of my blood on the floor. That must have been so hard for them.

"That makes sense. She doesn't seem the type to go back to the scene," I say, running my fingers through my hair. "But I don't think she's done with us yet."

"Me neither," Cooper says, butting in. He's our lore guy. He collects rare books that are filled with knowledge so whenever I have a question about the specifics of a creature, he's the guy I go to. "It would seem that the vampire we took out was her mate. If what I read about is true, I'm not sure she'll ever stop until she gets some sort of sick vengeance, Jeff."

I nod slowly. "I think you're right. She kept mentioning how she was going to make me hurt as much as she's hurting."

"Don't you think you've suffered enough?" Martin asks gently. Our gentle giant. The man knows all there is to know about weapons, including how to use them. Yet, is always there with a soft answer or listening ear.

"To her? Probably not."

"And how do you feel about this woman?" Cooper asks, his eyes never leaving mine. "Would you be okay with us taking care of her, Jeff?"

"I know what you're asking and no, I don't feel some debt to her for turning me into a vampire." I pause before adding, "I don't feel any sort of bond with her at all."

The hand on my shoulder squeezes. "That might be because you haven't seen her since your transformation," Axel says gently. "Sometimes the bond doesn't happen until you meet again after waking up."

"Fucking great," I murmur, rubbing at my eyes.

"It's alright," Carlos says, "you can't help it. None of us would hold it against you if we had to be the one to do the deed. All we care about is taking care of this and making sure you're safe."

"Alright, alright. I'm the one supposed to be taking care of you, kid, not the other way around."

Carlos shrugs. When the hell did he get so wise? He's the baby of our group yet here he is, making sure I'm safe and sound. I'm not sure I could be more proud. "Or. And hear me out. We could all take care of each other?"

The other guys around the table murmur their agreements, nodding their heads. Gods, I love my team.

I playfully give them all a dramatic sigh. *"Fine.* I guess you can all worry about me."

We continue on like always, laughing about the idiotic things we've done at past hunts, sharing some food, and just hanging out. It's refreshing, knowing that I haven't changed. I'm not a different person just because I'm a vampire now. This is still my family and they still love me.

Axel was right, this is exactly what I needed.

Before they all leave, I catalog them into my head, adding them to the senses I possess now. They all have their own unique scent and I file them away under *family.* "You smell like a wet dog," I blurt out when I hug Carlos, immediately regretting it as soon as I've said it. That's fucking rude.

Carlos gives the most awkward chuckle I think I've ever heard. "Must have been that dog I stopped to pet."

"Right," I murmur, not believing him for a second but

letting the topic drop. I look at everyone. "Please make sure no one is going out on their own. And make sure you have weapons on you at all times, just in case. I'm not sure what this woman's next move will be but I don't want any of us to be unprepared, alright?"

"You got it," Martin says, giving me one last hug before they're all on their way out the door, off to the campgrounds once more.

The moment they're all out, a pang of longing hits me full force. I want to be with them. I want to be in my camper. I want to be *useful* again.

But then my eyes meet Axel's and the longing turns into something else. Hope? Excitement? And maybe a tiny bit of trepidation about the unknowns of my-- no, *our* future.

I can't just think about me. I can't just think about my team. Now, I have *a mate* to consider. Would he even want me to continue being a hunter? I've never imagined my life outside of being a hunter. I can't imagine doing anything else.

How would I gain redemption from my past if I'm not doing good as a hunter?

Before I work myself into a full on panic, I take a deep breath, letting Axel's scent wash over me. The most important thing right now is to continue training my self-control and getting used to being in this body. Everything else will fall into place. That's what I have to hold on to.

CHAPTER TEN
AXEL

I LAY my feet in Jeff's lap, smiling to myself as his hand wraps around my ankle and squeezes. This has become a regular occurrence in this household. The gang's all here. Cooper is laying on the floor, a couple of books laid out in front of him. Ronny is on his laptop, typing away. Carlos and Jeff are playing a card game with Martin and I'm just here, taking everything in.

The search for the vampire that turned Jeff is still ongoing. Every time I think about it, my stomach sinks. She's keeping low and I have this sinking feeling that she's planning something.

Whatever it is, I have a feeling this team will be able to take care of it.

"Go fish," Martin says with an annoyed huff and I notice the way Cooper smiles to himself. I wonder if they have something going on. There's definitely *something* there, though they'd like everyone to believe they're some sort of rivals, but I can see through that. I hope I get to be in the front row to see them get their shit together someday.

I wiggle my toes against Jeff before moving so I can stand up. "Does anyone need refills?"

"Oh, I'll help you," Carlos says, standing up and setting his cards down.

"You're just mad you're losing," Jeff says with a warm chuckle.

"Oh yes," Carlos teases, his voice dripping with sarcasm, "I'll forever be devastated that I lost this game of go-fish."

I grab everyone's empty bottles on the way to the kitchen, dumping them into my recycling bin before heading to the fridge. "Do you want a soda or something?"

Carlos gives me a small smile, nodding his head. "Yeah, I'll just take whatever you have. I'm not picky."

I get to work pulling out new beers and a soda for Carlos, popping the tops off the beer bottles. I get one more for myself but Carlos clears his throat. I pause, looking over at him.

Carlos looks nervous, biting at his bottom lip and looking all sorts of unsure. I take a deep breath, trying to get a sense of what's going on based on scent, something I've been taught to do as a child. There are so many perks to being a vampire and this happens to be one of them.

He smells nervous. And like wet dog. It's a smell I noticed the very first time I met him but one I haven't brought up. None of the team seem to really know there's anything different about Carlos which isn't surprising since they don't have the heightened senses like I do, and if they do know, they don't care.

"What's up?"

He lets out a long sigh, touching his necklace. "I don't think you should be drinking that."

My stomach flips. I set the beer back into the fridge slowly, feeling embarrassed I'd even grabbed it. "It was more force of habit than anything. To fit in with the humans," I admit with a self-deprecating smile. There's something I've been ignoring for a couple weeks now, something I wasn't quite prepared to admit to myself.

"I wasn't sure if you knew or not," he says, his face bright red. "I umm," Carlos starts to say, cutting himself off with an awkward cough. "I may or may not have been able to hear the heartbeat."

"Do the rest know that you're not human?"

Carlos shrugs, rubbing at the back of his neck. "Honestly? I'm not entirely sure. Sometimes they say things that make me think they know, but I've never come out and said it before."

"Are you planning on telling them?"

"If I ever needed to I wouldn't lie. But I have no plans of renting a plane and putting it up in the sky."

I snort in amusement. "No one's asking you to do that."

"I know. It's just ironic, isn't it? Someone like me being a hunter."

"Isn't it ironic? A baby vampire leading a group of hunters."

Carlos finally cracks a smile. "Apparently Lady Fate

knew exactly the type of mate Jeff would need to put up with all of us."

My chest warms at the idea of me fitting in with Jeff's team. To fit into the little family he's created for himself. My hand goes to my stomach.

"How the fuck does a baby fit into a hunter's life?"

Carlos takes a long moment to answer. "I'm not entirely sure. But I know a hunter's hours are flexible, we can live anywhere, and we get to pick and choose which jobs we take. Jeff would never do anything to put you or the baby at risk, if that's what you're worried about."

"Not even a little bit. That never even crossed my mind. I'm more worried that Jeff will think he needs to pick the white picket fence life instead of hunting when that's the last thing I want for him."

"He's stubborn," Carlos says with a smile. "But he's also calculated. Reasonable. If you talk to him, I have no doubt you'll figure things out."

I reach over, squeezing Carlos' shoulder. "Thank you. You're very wise for being the baby of the group."

Carlos groans. "Not you too."

"I have to, Carlos," I say with a chuckle. "It's like a rite of passage. Let me have this."

"Fine," Carlos says, faking the most dramatic sigh and making me giggle a little more. He helps me bring everything into the living room, passing out everyone's drinks.

"Come here, baby," Jeff says when I step over to him. I go to sit next to him but let out a surprised noise when he grabs me around the waist and tugs me into his lap.

Jeff nuzzles the back of my neck and I can feel him

breathing me in. I wonder if he can smell the baby, smell that it's not just me anymore. Does he even realize the way he's been more affectionate lately? Are his instincts going crazy, telling him to protect me?

Gods, I really need to talk to him about this. Being a born vampire, I knew this was a possibility but I'd been ignoring it, not wanting to think about it.

The idea of Jeff going back to hunting scares me. Not because I don't trust him, because I do. I know he's strong and I've seen his self-control first hand, but I'm still scared. What if he comes up against something he can't fight his way out of? What if something happens to him and I'm left all alone, left with our baby?

My trust in Jeff is bigger than my fear though, so I'll continue to hold onto that.

He deserves to know the truth.

With my mind made up, I promise to talk to him about it tonight. Joy surges through me and a smile spreads across my lips. I turn my head in order to kiss Jeff on the lips, wanting him to feel the amount of affection I have for him. It doesn't matter it's been a mere few weeks since we've met. We're true mates and I know that means feelings grow quickly. I embrace them, just as much as I embrace Jeff.

"Alright, alright," Ronny calls out with a good natured laugh. "Save it for the bedroom. Sheeesh."

"Don't be such a prude," Cooper says back, looking up from his book. "You act like you've never seen someone kiss before. It hasn't been *that* long since you've gotten laid, has it, Ronny?"

Ronny's face turns bright red and he looks away. "Shut

it, Cooper," he says but even though the words are terse, I know there's nothing but love between all these guys.

I'm struck with emotions as I sit back against Jeff's chest. There's so much love here and somehow, Lady Fate has deemed me worthy to be a part of this family. I lace my fingers with Jeff's over the center of my belly. I can't wait to tell him about the life inside of me. I just hope that conversation goes well and that my anxieties are unwarranted.

CHAPTER ELEVEN
JEFF

AXEL'S BEEN off the last week.

Yes, I realize I've only known him a few weeks but during that time I truly do feel like I've gotten to know him. Well enough that I can notice when he's not exactly being himself. Call it hunter intuition, call it instincts, all I know is that something is different.

And that's without thinking about his scent. The smell of fresh rain is heightened with new notes to it. Something like lilacs or honey are mixed in there. It's delicious and new and making my brain absolutely melt with emotions that I don't quite understand.

At this point, I've started to get used to my instincts. They pop up at random times. Instincts to protect Axel, or to call Carlos and check in on him, or needing to wear Axel's clothes so his scent is close to me.

Once everyone has been ushered out of our home, I tug Axel close. I ignore the way I've started calling this place my home. It's not necessarily this apartment, I realize, but the place I share *with Axel*. He's my home now. Wherever he is that is where I'll be.

I run my thumb over his cheek softly, my stomach swooping when he smiles up at me. Gods, I can't even begin to describe the feelings welling up inside of me. They're all consuming until I'm completely caught ablaze, burning away the selfish parts of myself and focusing on Axel and being the best partner I can be for him.

The vampire in front of me is kind, and funny, and beautiful. It truly must have been an act of Lady Fate to orchestrate this meeting because there's no way it happened by chance.

I lean down and kiss Axel's lips. His hands go around my middle, holding me tight. My stomach swoops with affection. I didn't even know it was possible to fall for someone this quickly. Maybe it's because we're true mates, maybe it's because I'm a vampire, or maybe it's just *Axel*. I don't care what it is, I just care about Axel. And I care about him knowing how I feel.

Maybe if he knows I'm in this with both feet, it'll help whatever's going on inside his head this last week.

"I have plans for you," I murmur against Axel's lips, feeling the way they split into a smile.

"Oh yeah?"

"Mhmm. Very good plans. The best really. Would you like to hear about them?"

There's a moment of hesitation. "I should really talk to you about something first."

I pull back, running my nose gently over his before nodding slowly. "Okay, baby. You can talk to me about anything, okay?" I take his hand, leading him over to the couch and sitting down. My thumb runs over his knuckles, wanting him to know I'm here, that we're connected. My eyes glance up at the mating bite on his throat, a flutter of possession going through me at the sight.

"This is going to be a bit of a shock," Axel murmurs, looking self-conscious and worried.

"More shocking than waking up a vampire?"

Axel finally cracks the smallest smile, his eyes meeting mine. "It's gonna be about the same level I think," he says carefully. "I'm not sure if I've explicitly said this but I'm a born vampire."

"Okay," I say slowly, "I already knew that."

"Great. One less thing to explain. Umm, so there are some things born vampires can do that bitten ones cannot."

"I read about this," I tell him, proud of myself for the research I've done. "They don't have the same ties that turned vampires have which is kinda nice. And they're able to have babies with their mates. I read about all of this in the books that Cooper let me borrow. It's kinda fascinating."

"Right," Axel says and when our eyes meet, my stomach clenches. He's staring at me, willing me to under-stand something that's apparently flying over my head. I think back to this conversation, to what I've said.

"I'm sorry, baby, but I'm still not getting it. You're gonna have to spell it out for me."

Axel lets out a long breath, shaking his head at me. But it's a playful look, not one of real frustration. "I'm surprised you haven't picked up on the signs yet," he says, taking my hand and bringing it to his stomach. "Listen, Jeff."

I close my eyes and focus on *listening*. There's someone walking outside, their boots clicking against the sidewalk. There are birds chirping on a nearby branch. A twig snaps. I focus closer. There. I tilt my head, really listening. What is that?

I open my eyes and look at Axel. "There's like a weird whumping sound? What is that?"

Axel full on rolls his eyes at me. "Oh my gods," he murmurs before squeezing my wrist. "The sound is coming from in there."

I stare at him a long moment before it hits me. *Oh.* Oh wow. Holy shit. Okay.

"You're pregnant?"

Axel nods his head slowly, gauging my reaction. He looks nervous and that's the last feeling he should be happening. I smile so wide my cheeks hurt before pulling him into my lap, wrapping my arms around him tight and burying my face against his throat. I hold him for a long time.

Holy shit. I'm going to be a dad. That wasn't something I'd let myself think about. Children aren't really something I let myself hope for because I'm a hunter. My job is dangerous and scary and one wrong turn I would leave that kid without a dad.

Can I even keep hunting? Should I give up this life?

Holy shit.

"Are you upset?"

I pull back, looking up into Axel's eyes. "Far from it," I

tell him seriously. I touch his cheek gently and he leans into my touch. "I'm overwhelmed but not in a bad way." I tug Axel down, kissing his lips softly. "I'm happy, baby."

"You are?"

"Yes. We're gonna have a baby. We're gonna have a child together. A family. It's so much, but I'm also so, so happy, Axel."

Axel's fingers run through my hair. "I'm happy too. I never dreamed of meeting my true mate but now you're *here*. You're so *good*, Jeff. A hunter who takes care of those weaker than you. I admire you so much and I couldn't be more proud that our baby will have a father like you."

I feel my throat tighten at Axel's words. "How can I be a hunter and a dad?" I ask the questions rattling inside of me.

Axel gives a small shrug. "I have no idea but I know we'll figure it out. I can live in the RV. Or we can buy some different places around the country as home bases."

"With what money? Hunting doesn't really pay the bills, baby," I say with a self-depreciating huff.

"Oh, umm, I can take care of that," Axel says. "My fathers made sure I would want for nothing. They've been alive a long time and invested. I'm what the kids would call a trust fund baby."

"Wait. Hold on," I say, a grin spreading across my lips. "You're my sugar daddy?"

Axel slaps my shoulder, letting out a giggle. "Shut it, Jeff. I'm just saying we can make this work. As long as you *want* to make it work?"

"Very much so," I say without even needing to think about it. "I can't imagine you raising this baby without me by your side. It won't be a conventional family or home, but it'll be *ours*." Already, I can see it. Home bases all over the country and taking jobs close by, moving from house to house, having a place for the crew to park their RVs at. The plan is already forming in my brain and I love it.

I love *him*.

Which is why he deserves to know the whole truth. "I've never told you about my family," I say slowly, holding onto Axel's hand and leaning on his strength."

"You don't have to tell me anything you don't want to, Jeff."

"I want to tell you," I say right away, taking a steadying breath. "I come from a hunting family. My mom and dad taught me and my sister everything there was to know about the lifestyle."

Axel tugs my hand up and kisses my knuckles. "That must have been a really hard childhood," he whispers.

"You'd think, but we were still allowed to be kids. We played and traveled and would often stay with random relatives while our parents worked. We didn't even realize the truth of what was happening until we were older. My sister and I started training as a team. We were insepara-ble." A pang of longing hits me straight in the chest. I missed that. Missed having her in my pocket, anticipating my moves before I even did them. I miss my sister.

"But something changed when we became adults," I continue on, wishing this wasn't so hard. I thought with time it would be easier but it hasn't. "She started dating this guy. He was really nice to her and had a twin brother. I thought things were going well."

When I pause, Axel whispers, "what happened?"

I clear my throat, looking away. "My sister went rogue. She killed the guy's parents. And then she tried to kill him and his brother."

"Oh gods," Axel murmurs, covering his mouth with his hand.

"Yeah," I say humorlessly. "It was awful. She died that night. The guy was a *dragon* shifter and she *thankfully* wasn't prepared. When I found her, my parents took her side instead of seeing how fucking wrong it was for her to hunt anyone that wasn't human."

Axel carefully crawls into my lap, holding my face between his hands. "You do not have to pay for the sins of your sister," he says and all the air leaves my lungs in one deep sigh. Emotions well up inside of me. I want to fight him so badly because I deserve to hurt for her sins. I should have seen the signs. I should have stopped her.

But I hold onto his words with everything I have inside of me. I hold onto them and fucking *pray* that someday I'll believe them.

"That's why my team lives by a code," I whisper, my voice much softer now that Axel is in my lap. I meet his pretty brown eyes, willing him to understand.

"You're a good man, Jeff. You are *good*. Redemption isn't a thing you need to earn because you haven't done the wrong. But it's admirable that you live by a code and shield humans from danger."

I rest my forehead against the center of his chest, letting him run his fingers through my hair. I am so in love with this man.

These few weeks have been so fucking hard, learning self-control, learning to drink blood without letting the hunger consume me, learning about my instincts and feelings. But being with Axel has been so *easy*. Being with him is like breathing. We belong together.

It might have been a short time but already I know I can't go back to what it was like not having him in my life. I can't go back to not having him near.

I love him.

I take Axel's hand, bringing it to my mouth and kissing each of his fingers. My fangs slide down and Axel sucks in a sharp breath that makes me smile.

I don't say the words. Not yet. But I *do* take Axel to our bedroom and show him my feelings with gentle kisses, soothing touches, and soft, murmured words. My wonderful mate. My soul mate. My baby's father.

I love him and I promise to protect him, to love him, and to make sure he never questions my feelings for him.

CHAPTER TWELVE
AXEL

I REACH OVER and thread my fingers with Jeff's, squeezing his hand. "You're doing so well, Jeff."

He gives me a quick nod. His body is stiff and he's not even breathing. We're outside. We're walking towards the local campground to meet up with the crew and Jeff is stiff as a board because people are walking towards us.

"You can do this. Just keep holding my hand and focusing on me."

"I can do this," he says, his voice strained. "You won't let me hurt them, right?"

"I would never let that happen," I tell him seriously. "If I didn't think you could do this, we'd still be at the apartment. But I *know* you can do this."

"Plus I just ate before we left. I'm super full. It wouldn't even be worth eating someone because I wouldn't enjoy it."

I let out a surprised snort. "Oh my gods," I blurt out, looking over at Jeff in surprise. He's smirking back at me.

"You're ridiculous," I tell him with a giggle and he

chuckles back. As we pass the other couple, there's a moment when Jeff squeezes my hand but otherwise, nothing else happens.

Jeff lets out a long breath before looking at me. "Okay. So. That wasn't as bad as I thought it was gonna be."

"Not to be that guy *but,* I told you so."

Jeff looks over at me, making a silly face. His voice goes super high as he teases me, *"not to be that guy but I told you so."*

We walk hand in hand all the way to the campground with no further distractions or seeing anyone else. I breathe in the fresh air and smile to myself. Living in the woods like this sounds really nice. I've been in this same apartment for a while now, so leaving to explore the country doesn't sound like a bad idea. It actually sounds exciting. And I can easily train someone else to take care of the local blood bank here. I wonder if Angus, a vampire that lives around here with her two mates, would be interested in the job.

I run my free hand over my little bump. Plus, traveling the country will make our baby's life more interesting. They'll be able to see the world with their trusted family by their side. The more I think about it, the more I'm on board for this new chapter of my life.

"What the hell did those assholes do?"

Our steps slow down as we find the campsite. There are three campers parked in a half circle. The one in the middle has little lanterns hung from the outside with a welcome home streamer across the door.

"Awwww," I coo, looking around with a wide smile. "This is adorable!"

"This is so embarrassing."

"It's not! They care about you, Jeff. It's so sweet."

Jeff continues to grumble but I can see the glint in his eyes. He loves this. As we step inside, I somehow smile even wider. There are two glasses on the table waiting for us and I can smell its blood. There's fake candles lit all over and the whole place smells freshly cleaned. Everyone is gone, apparently leaving us this little gift.

"So," I say slowly, stepping over to the table and picking up one of the glasses. "This is your camper. It's nice, Jeff."

"Thanks," he says, picking up his own glass and pulling me past a sheet that's hung up, dividing the rest of the camper from the bedroom.

There's more fake candles in here along with some rose petals on the bed. "Would it be rude to umm?"

Jeff's eyes darken and he smirks. "I think it would be rude *not* to. Like throwing away a gift, right?"

I giggle before drinking all of my blood quickly. I set the cup down before crawling onto the bed. "Well then, come here and properly show me your bed."

I sit back against his pillows, watching as he gulps the blood down. His Adam's apple bobs with each gulp and the tiniest drop escapes, dripping from the side of his mouth down to his throat. Fuck, I want to lick it up before feeding it back into his mouth for him.

"Come on," I say, not disguising the whine in my voice. I'm suddenly overwhelmed with my need for my mate. I want him so fucking badly. I start to shimmy out of my clothes, wanting to be naked and unconstructed by these clothes.

After finishing his cup of blood, Jeff quickly strips out of his own clothes. Gods, I'll never get tired of seeing my mate naked with all that toned, strong, pale skin. If we weren't vampires, I would leave so many marks against that skin just so I could see it for days afterwards. But we are vampires, so instead I'll leave bites that'll fade by tomorrow.

"Jeff, if you don't get your ass in this bed--" my words are cut off with a grunt as he leaps into the bed. Our lips connect in a sloppy kiss that's filled with giggles. I love this. I love that we can have so much fun together. I love that we can also be serious when we need to be. We fit.

"I'd really like to suck your dick," Jeff says against my lips, his voice sounding impossibly deep, filled with lust.

"Yes," I breathe out. "Please, Jeff. Turn around. Don't want you feeling left out."

Jeff quickly readjusts until he's facing my cock, his ass hovering over my face. My plan was to suck his dick at the same time as he was sucking mine but with his pale ass here? Well, I just couldn't resist such a pretty sight.

"Oh my *gods*," Jeff yelps out, his body breaking out with goosebumps. I pull his ass back until I can get my mouth on him. I nip playfully at his ass cheek, letting him know what I have planned. "I've never."

"Do you not want me to?"

"I do. I really fucking do," Jeff says and my cock twitches, knowing my mouth will be the first *and the last* to ever touch his ass.

Jeff's hands touch my belly and my heart stutters. My belly is starting to pouch out with a bump and Jeff seems to *love* it. He gets all possessive whenever he sees it and right now is no different. "Mine," he says as he leans down and kisses just above my belly button before wrapping his hand around my cock.

A whine leaves my lips and my hips come up off the bed, chasing his touch. "This is mine. You're *mine*, Axel."

"Yours," I breathe. I couldn't agree more. I'm his just as he is mine.

I dig my fingers into Jeff's ass before pulling his cheeks apart. I don't give him time to prepare or overthink. Without warning, I dive in, licking across his crack. Jeff's body tenses up before he's moaning, the sound filling me with satisfaction and lust.

I take my time, licking over his hole, swirling my tongue around in little circles. My fingers tighten against Jeff's skin as I pleasure him with my tongue.

A gasp leaves my lips and I pull back for a moment as Jeff takes my cock into his mouth. His mouth is so *warm* and wet around me. It feels so good. "Jeff. Fuck," I groan out, thrusting my hips up only to have him hold me down.

Why is that so fucking hot?

He sucks me down, making my toes curl in pleasure. Jeff takes his time, teasing the head of my cock with his tongue before taking all of me into his mouth and down his throat. Gods, I could sit back and enjoy this all night. But maybe another night, because right now I have the most perfect ass to eat right in front of my face.

I quickly dive back in, giving as much pleasure as Jeff is giving to me, wanting him to feel good. The noises he makes as he sucks on my cock tells me I'm doing just that, his moans vibrating through me. I point my tongue, wiggling it against his hole until it grows soft and pliant. I bring one of my hands to my mouth, spitting on my fingers before touching Jeff's hole.

"Oh gods," he gasps out, his hips pushing back against me, begging for me to push inside. I give him exactly what he wants. "Yes, Axel. Fuck. Keep going."

"Wouldn't dream of stopping," I tell him, nipping his ass cheek just to hear him gasp.

I push my finger inside, watching in wonder as his body takes me in with ease. I finger him slowly, enjoying the desperate noises he makes, begging me for more. Jeff doubles his efforts, sucking my cock into his throat and holding me there. Another perk of being a vampire and not needing to breathe.

"Fuck, Jeff! You're gonna make me come!"

"That's the point," he murmurs and I can hear the smirk in his voice. It feels like Jeff is trying to suck my brain right out of my dick and if I'm honest, this is not a bad way to go.

As two of my fingers fuck into Jeff's ass, trying my best to run over his prostate, I run my nose over the back of his thigh. Yes. Right here. This spot is perfect. He'll be feeling it all night, thinking about how good I made him feel.

I let my fangs drop down, licking over their sharp edge before opening wide and biting down on the back of Jeff's thigh. The whine he lets out makes a shiver run down my spine. His body tenses with pleasure and I can feel the way his cock twitches where it touches my chest.

Blood pools in my mouth and I close my eyes, savoring the flavor and feel of it. Pleasure is pooling hotly in my gut and I'm so close to my orgasm. Jeff's fingers tighten against my hips and the bit of pain is mixing with my pleasure.

My fingers pick up speed. Jeff's hips start moving, thrusting his cock against my chest before riding back onto my fingers. Gods, he's chasing his pleasure and it's incredibly sexy. I'm close. I'm so close. Just a little more.

Jeff's body tenses and his ass clamps down around my fingers. A moment later, the smell of his cum hits my nose as warm, wetness splatters across my chest. Fuck!

My orgasm crashes over me, making lightning bolts run down my spine. My cock throbs and twitches, emptying into Jeff's mouth. I dig my teeth into Jeff's skin just a little harder, sucking one more time before letting go and licking the leftover blood away.

"Fuck," I whisper, overwhelmed with how *good* my body feels after that orgasm. Jeff leans his forehead against my thigh, no doubt feeling the same. I gently pull my fingers free, giving his ass cheek one last peck before pushing his hip.

Jeff quickly moves around, flopping down onto his back and pulling me close to his chest. His fingers find my chest, swirling through the cooling cum he's left there.

I wrinkle my nose at him. "Eww."

"No eww," he says right away with a bright smile. "Sexy. Marked you. Now everyone will know you're mine."

"Jeff," I say with a little giggle. "Your family can't even smell this. They're human."

Jeff shrugs. "I don't care. Let me have this."

I pull him into a kiss, smiling against his lips. "You can have this. You can have all of me."

"Promise?"

"Of course," I murmur, kissing him again. I'm talking around the one point I want him to know and in this moment, after coming so hard I saw stars, with Jeff still rubbing his cum into my skin, I can't stop myself from blurting it out. "I'm your true mate. I'm not going anywhere. Plus, I love you."

Jeff's hand stills. His eyes are wide as they meet mine. "You love me?"

I nod my head slowly, my chest clenching. "I do. You're everything I've always wanted in a partner. You make me want to explore and try new things. You're so strong and so loyal. And you're *good*, Jeff. You do so much good for our world. Plus you've given me a family with your crew." I kiss him one more time just to solidify my points. "I love you, Jeff."

Jeff's eyes are huge, hanging on every single one of my words. Finally, he lets out a long breath. "I don't feel like I deserve you."

"You do. You deserve all of me just like I deserve all of you."

This time it's Jeff who initiates the kiss. His tongue touches my own, the kiss fierce as he pours his love into the kiss. When he pulls back, he gently runs his nose over mine. "I love you too. I'm doing my best to believe that I deserve this, but it's hard. I feel like I have so much to redeem myself for still."

"You can keep hunting for redemption if you feel the need to, but I'm here to remind you that you're *good*. The sins of your past don't define you, Jeff. *You* define who you are. And I love who you are."

Jeff pulls me until we're pressed together, holding each other tight. He kisses the top of my head as my lids grow heavy and my limbs all go limp, the orgasm catching up to me.

"I love you so much," he whispers into my hair, and it's the last thing I hear before I fall asleep.

CHAPTER THIRTEEN
AXEL

"GOOD MORNING!"

I wrap my shirt tighter around my middle, letting out a little yawn as I step out of the RV. "Good morning," I call over to Carlos.

The morning air is cool and crisp. I breathe it in, letting a smile play at my lips. I haven't moved all my things out here, but I have been sleeping in the RV for about a couple weeks now. It's nice, waking up and stepping outside into nature each morning. It's also been nice to spend more time with Jeff's crew, and getting to know them and letting them get to know me.

They're a good bunch of guys but I expect no less. Their leader is a good man, it makes sense Jeff would surround himself with good people in turn.

"Did you sleep well?"

I nod, stepping over to where he's sitting. "I did, thanks. You?" Carlos gives me a thumbs up in answer. "Do you wanna go for a walk with me? I was thinking of heading down to the campground office and seeing if they have some instant coffee."

"Yeah, I'll come along. Can't have you walking around by yourself."

A flutter of worry goes through me, like a bucket of cold water. I know the rules. Nobody wanders anywhere alone, we all travel with buddies. I hate that we have to be so cautious. I hate that we still don't know where Jeff's sire is and what her plans are.

I wish she'd just make her move already. I'm tired of sitting around and waiting. I want to live my life without this particular worry shadowing my enjoyment. The dread that fills me every time I hear a branch snap is getting old and I want this to be over once and for all.

Carlos stands up, stretching his hands over his head before stepping next to me. We make our way down the winding pavement towards the campground office.

"I'm glad you can still hide your belly with big sweaters," Carlos says, nodding down to my stomach. "Pretty soon you'll be stuck at the campsite."

I let out a dramatic groan. "Don't remind me. Sometimes I wish the world knew about us, just so we wouldn't have to hide certain things," I tell him, shaking my head. "But then I remember how humans can be and decided it's probably for the best."

"Yeah," Carlos says with a wince, "sometimes they don't do well with large changes. Hearing about the supernatural world might not go over as well as we hope."

Just as the office comes into view, a noise catches my attention. With lightning speed, something runs right into

Carlos. He lets out a pained noise before he's falling to the ground. Bright, red blood pools around his throat where a new bite is and my stomach sinks all the way down to my feet.

"Fuck," I gasp out, turning and running. But I'm too slow. Something clips my feet and I hit the pavement. My hands and knees lance with stinging pain. "Fuck!"

Boots click against the pavement and I look up to find a woman standing over me. Fear strikes me deeper than I've ever felt before and my entire body goes cold. "There you are," she murmurs, leaning down and grabbing my wrist, yanking me up to my feet.

I open my mouth to scream, praying that one of the guys will hear me but she's faster, shoving something into my mouth to keep me quiet.

I look down at Carlos, thankful that his chest is still moving. His shifter body will heal before he bleeds out. He'll be okay. That thought is the only happy thing I can think of and I cling to that, letting it give me a sliver of hope.

"Off we go," she murmurs, yanking me along. The further we get away from the campground, the more bile rises up in my throat. I might actually throw up.

"Where are we going?" I murmur as best as I can around the material in my mouth.

"Don't worry about it. I'm sorry that you got tangled up in the middle of this," she says, her voice coming out in harsh pants, her skin somehow even paler than a vampire's should be. She looks *sick*. "You're just an innocent sap who got the unfortunate luck to be mated to a killer."

Before I can stop myself I hiss out, *"you're* the killer! You were killing innocent people!"

"Shut up," she snaps, letting out a hiss of her own. I instantly stand down, knowing she can't be reasoned with. She's crazed with the need for vengeance. "Humans are *food*. He killed *my mate*. He has to pay. He has too. He has to know how hurt I am," she starts to say, her words drifting in and out and her eyes darting every which way.

There's no getting through to her. Which makes this entire situation that much more terrifying. When I thought there was hope of talking my way out of this, I was okay, holding onto that. But now? Now I know just how fucking screwed I am.

The grip around my arm tightens until I'm crying out in pain. She just snorts, shaking her head like it's amusing to hurt me. I understand she was hurt, but to go to this length to hurt Jeff back? Not only to take away his humanity but then take away his *true mate* as well? She's a lost cause.

Will she wait to kill me until Jeff arrives so he has to witness it?

Gods I hope not.

Tears prickle behind my eyes. All I can do is hope that Jeff and his crew are just as good as they say they are. I have to trust their ability to find me and stop this woman. After all the stories I've heard, they truly do sound like super-heroes. Now it's time for them to prove it.

CHAPTER FOURTEEN
JEFF

I WAKE UP SLOWLY, reaching out for Axel instinctively and frowning when my hand comes up empty. I open my eyes, finding the morning sun already streaming in through the windows of my RV. I blurrily blink the morning dust away, trying to shake myself fully awake.

What I wouldn't give for a hot cup of blood coffee this morning.

With a final yawn, I get myself up and out of bed. I change out of my pajamas and into my day clothes quickly before heading outside. I take a deep breath, letting the cool morning air further wake me up.

Martin is already out here, starting up the fire so we can cook some breakfast. I give him a small smile, pulling up a chair and sinking into it with a sigh. I'm not sure why but I feel like I'm in a funk this morning. There's a pit gnawing its way into my belly.

My eyes dart all around the forest around us, wondering if there's something out there putting me on guard. Are these my instincts? Or is this just a weird feeling after waking up without my mate in bed with me?

I shift in my seat, clearing my throat. "Have you seen Axel this morning?"

Martin shakes his head. "I think he went for a walk with Carlos." My brows wrinkle and there's something rising up inside my chest, something close to panic. What the fuck is going on? "What's up? Is something wrong?"

"I'm--" I start to say, shaking my head, trying to clear it. "I'm not sure. Just, something feels off."

Martin sets his supplies down, standing up. "Do you wanna go look for them? Just to be sure?"

I think about it for a moment. "I'm not sure," I confess softly, feeling somewhat out of my league at the moment. How do you explain to someone your insides are welling up with panic without any reason? I stand up, running my fingers through my hair. "Okay, yeah. There's nothing wrong with bothering them, just to make sure they're okay."

"You're not bothering them," Martin says, reaching over and patting my shoulder when I make my way over to him. "You're checking in on your true mate. From what I've gathered, having one of those is a huge deal." He gives a shrug. "Nothing wrong with making sure they're okay."

"Yeah, you're right," I say, giving him a little smile.

Just as we're stepping onto the path leading up to the campground office, the smell of blood hits my nose. My body goes cold all over and tense with panic. "I smell blood," I blurt out, preparing myself to run full speed ahead. But before I can, I see Carlos running towards us.

"What the fuck," Martin murmurs, stepping ahead of me and catching Carlos in his arms. "What the fuck happened, kid?"

Carlos is clutching the side of his throat, blood still sluggishly pouring from what I can clearly see is a bite. Thank gods I don't need to breathe because right now I don't think I could even if I needed it. My head is throbbing with panic and my vision is starting to blur. Where's Axel? Where the fuck is my mate?

"Vampire," Carlos grits out, holding his throat. "She got the jump on me. I'm so sorry," he says, his voice filled with anguish. "She took Axel."

That sparks me into action. "We have to tell the others." I shake my head. "No, you two get back to camp, have Ronny track Axel's phone. Maybe she's sloppy and left it on him. I'll start tracking his scent." I take out my ear piece, thankful I grabbed it this morning and slipped it into my pocket.

"You can't go alone," Martin says, looking worried. "Who knows what she has planned. You need backup."

I shake my head, putting my ear piece into place. "I'm a *vampire*, Martin. You won't be able to keep up with me. Once Ronny's located the place Axel is being held, you're free to come join. But right now I'm going to run after Axel's scent." I give him the smallest smile, "if you want we can race and see who finds him first."

It has the wanted effect, sparking a tiny bit of hope in Martin. I pretend to feel it too instead of the overwhelming rage that's taking over. Someone's taken *my mate*. Someone is trying to hurt my mate and my baby, and I won't let them get away with this.

My instincts want blood. And as a hunter, I'm inclined to follow that instinct wholeheartedly.

"Go," I tell Martin. "And don't beat yourself up, kid," I say to Carlos, not liking the look he's giving me. "It wasn't your fault. We'll get Axel back."

He nods back. Once I know they're on their way back, I stop holding myself back. An animalist hiss leaves my chest as I run down the pavement. I find the spot Axel was taken, can smell Carlos' blood thick in the air. If he wasn't my family, I know the scent would be distracting me, make my mouth water and my fangs drop. But his blood has too much wet dog to it to be appealing.

I take a deep breath and close my eyes, parsing out the scents around me. There's the smell of forest and moss, of Carlos' blood, but *there*, that's solely Axel's scent. I hold onto it, finding the thread of it and chasing it.

Before I even realize what's happening, my feet are moving, chasing after the smell of fresh rain. The path feels incredibly straightforward, like this woman didn't care about covering up their tracks. Was she too focused on finally having Axel to care about me following her?

"Bossman?" comes in through my earpiece.

"I hear you loud and clear," I say back to Ronny.

"The phone is still," he tells me before rattling off an address. My stomach sinks. It's the same place I killed her mate. Fuck.

"I have a bad feeling," I say slowly, never stopping my movement forward. With the address in mind, it's even easier to follow Axel's scent, knowing exactly where it'll lead me. "Why is she being so sloppy? She didn't cover her tracks at all."

"It's almost like she wants you to show up."

I swallow thickly. "That's what I'm afraid of."

"Don't think like that," Ronny says right away and I can hear his fingers flying over the keys of his keyboard. "Stay positive, Jeff. You'll get there in time."

I nod despite the fact that Ronny can't see me. I can hear movement and a moment later, Martin is coming online with me, his voice in my ear alongside Ronny's. They might not physically be here with me but they're on my side, they have my back. It renews my strength and resolve. We'll get to Axel in time.

Axel's scent leads me to the warehouse. The doors are closed but not locked. Everything inside of me is screaming at me that this is a trap but I can't stop right now, not when I know Axel is just beyond these doors, waiting for me to save him.

I take only a second to compose myself before opening the door and walking inside. It's dingy and run down in here. I look at the ground, finding two sets of fresh footprints. One from the woman and another from Axel.

"You don't have to pull them so tight," I hear Axel say and I follow the sound of his voice, like a beacon leading my way. "It's not like I'm going anywhere."

"Shut up," the woman hisses out and my back stiffens. She sounds different than the last time we met. Before she was calm, collected. She knew exactly what she was doing. This time she sounds completely out of control.

"Found them," I breathe, wanting the guys to know I'm here.

"Be safe, Jeff. I'm three minutes out. I'll be there as fast as I can to have your back," Martin says into my ear. "And don't be afraid to do what you need to do to keep your mate safe."

If my heart could beat, I know it would be hammering a bruise into the inside of my chest. My steps are silent as I go.

"I know you're here." I go completely still, my entire body locking up. "I can smell you."

There goes my element of surprise. I step out into the open, no longer needing to hide. My eyes lock with Axel's and I do my best to silently tell him that everything is going to be okay. I'm here to save him.

I look over at the woman who's done so much damage in the small amount of time I've known her. Her eyes are still dark, filled with hate, but this time they're foggy. She's losing control of herself.

A pang goes through my chest. If only I could help her, if only I could save her. I pity her. I wish I didn't have to kill her. If given the chance, my stomach clenches because I wonder if I'll even be able to do it. Will I hesitate?

I clench my hands into tight fists, trying to clear my head. Are these even my own thoughts or is this the sire bond? Fuck, I feel all tied up inside. I freeze in place. In my line of work, hesitation usually gets you killed.

"Look at the gift I've given you," the woman says, giving me a wide smile that's filled with malice. The look makes a shiver run down my spine, especially combined with the blood that's drying across her mouth. No doubt that blood belongs to Carlos. "You're faster. You're stronger. You have supernatural instincts now. You're welcome."

I let out a hiss of annoyance, uncaring that my fangs are dropped or that I so obviously don't sound human. "I have nothing to thank you for."

"Nothing, huh?" She steps behind Axel, running her fingers over his shoulders. The way he tenses up makes me see red. *Mine. Mate. Intruder.* Instincts are shouting at me to make this woman stop, to have her not touch what's mine. But at the same time, there's a pull inside my gut, telling me to protect her. Gods, I hate this. I feel like pulling out my own hair.

"Don't fucking touch him."

"You can thank me for bringing you to your true mate. Isn't it wonderful? That bond you share with them? It's beautiful." Her eyes turn even darker and I startle, watching as the whites completely disappear, filling with dark red. "You took that away from me!"

"You were killing humans," I tell her. "I couldn't let him keep hurting people."

"Humans are *below* us," she says, like it makes complete sense. "They're our *food*."

"They're innocent people!"

Instead of responding, she lets out an inhuman snarl. I start to move but I know I'll be too slow. That hesitation is going to be the death of my true mate and I know without a doubt that I'll never be able to forgive myself.

But Axel moves faster.

Just as the woman is diving down to bite Axel's throat,

he tosses his head back, connecting with her nose. She lets out a scream, distracted. This is my chance and I refuse to not take it.

With my heightened speed, within the blink of an eye I'm behind her. I have no weapon. I have no gun. So I use the only thing I'm equipped with; following instincts I didn't even know I had, my nails grow into sharp points. Sharp enough to piece skin.

A sickening sound rings through the room as my hand goes through this woman's back. In my hand, I hold her heart. With a quick jerk, I pull it free from her chest. She turns to look at me with wide eyes, like she's in shock. And maybe she is. Her eyes meet mine before they dart down to my hand where her heart lies. After another excruciating moment, she crumbles to the ground.

I stare down at my hand. This woman's heart is in my hand, blood dripping down my fingers onto the floor. My mouth waters. The bloodlust is clouding my head, making it hard to focus on anything but her heart. *Drip. Drip. Drip.*

It would be so easy to bring it to my lips. It would be so easy to drink from it, to eat the flesh, to have this warm inside my belly. I want it. My fangs *ache* with how much I want it.

"Jeff?" I let out a hiss, taking a step back. My eyes meet Martin's and I freeze. "Hey," he whispers, holding up his hands in surrender. My eyes follow the movement until I'm looking over Martin's shoulder, right into some glass.

I see my reflection and my stomach sinks. Like cold water is thrown over my head. I look like a monster. My eyes are the same bloodshot red as the woman's, my fangs on full display. There's blood dripping from my hand that's holding a literal heart.

I drop the heart like I've been burned.

Oh gods.

I close my eyes, trying to find the self-control that Axel has taught me. I take a steadying breath, focusing on the smell of fresh rain, focusing on *Axel*. I can do this. I can remember how to be Jeff rather than the monster I've become.

When I open my eyes again, the red is gone, leaving my usual eyes. Martin relaxes, putting his hands back down. I can hear him murmuring into his ear piece that he's found us and that we're both okay.

I quickly fall to my knees before Axel, untying him. "I'm so sorry," I murmur, feeling utterly devastated that I've somehow let this happen. "I'm so sorry, Axel."

"Hey, hey," he murmurs, his hands going to my hair the moment they're untied. "This is *not* your fault, Jeff. You *saved* me. I knew you'd come for me."

I look up at him. "I will *always* come for you."

"I know you will. I'm so proud of you. Not only did you save me but you stopped yourself, Jeff. You could have let yourself lose control, but you didn't."

"Only just barely," I say under my breath, helping Axel to stand before lifting him off his feet and carrying him bridal style in my arms.

"Shush. It doesn't matter. All that matters is that I'm safe and you didn't lose control. Focus on the good for once, Jeff."

"He's right," Martin says, getting into step with me.

"You did good today, bossman." Then shyly he adds, "if that were me, I don't think I would have been able to stop."

"I wouldn't have if it weren't for you coming in."

"That's why we're a team," he tells me seriously. "When one of us is ready to give up, there's another one of us there to pick up the pieces and push each other on. That's what family is for."

Axel tucks his face against the underside of my neck, breathing me in. With him safe in my arms I feel like I can breathe again. When we eventually get back to the campground, Ronny and Cooper are there to receive us, checking up on both Axel and I to make sure we're okay.

"Where's Carlos?" Axel asks, looking around for him.

"Sleeping," Cooper says with a frown. "He didn't take this whole situation very well. Give him some time to recover."

"He's not blaming himself, is he?"

Cooper shrugs. "You know he is," he says in a hushed tone. "Plus, the blood loss has him tired as hell. I've sent him to bed once we knew you were safe."

Axel tightens his arms around himself. "I'll talk with him in the morning. He needs to know this wasn't his fault. We can't control what other people do, only how we react and he did the right thing. He got help the moment he could."

I keep Axel tucked tight against my side. "You're right. But sometimes that's not an easy lesson to learn."

He looks up at me, giving me a knowing look. "One that you could learn as well."

After everyone has given Axel a tight hug, I pull him

into my RV, needing to hold him. Under the safety of the blankets with his head against my chest, I finally let myself process what the fuck just happened.

"I almost lost you today," I murmur, my voice just barely audible. "I would have never forgiven myself."

"The same way you don't forgive yourself of your family's crimes?"

"Jesus, Axel. Give a guy a break. We just went through something traumatic!"

Axel tightens his arms around me. "If you're still searching for redemption, consider it granted in my eyes," he says after a moment. He leans up on his elbows in order to place a chaste kiss against my lips.

"You really think so?"

"Yes," he says without even needing to think about it. "Without a doubt."

I don't say anything more. We lapse into silence and after a little bit, I can feel Axel fall asleep. I stay awake a long time, thinking about what Axel said. He's my true mate, the one who's supposed to complete me. I love him more than words can say and somehow, he sees me as someone who doesn't need redemption.

Could I believe him?

I'm not sure, but in this moment I decide I'm going to try.

CHAPTER FIFTEEN
AXEL

THE LAST FEW months have gone by in what feels like a flash. One moment, I'm answering a call from Dakota and the next, I'm impatiently waiting for my baby to be born. It's incredible how fast Lady Fate moves when she brings two people together.

I'm so thankful she's brought Jeff into my life. I can't imagine going back to how things were before he was here. I wasn't necessarily lonely. But I longed for what I have now. I longed to be loved and cared for. I longed for adventure and trying new things. What's more adventurous and new than traveling with a bunch of hunters?

Jeff's been glued to my side ever since I was kidnapped. I don't blame him. His poor instincts must be going into overdrive the closer I get to delivering this baby. I wake up from nightmares once in a while, dreaming about what would have happened if Jeff hadn't arrived when he did, but mostly, I've adjusted just fine. Life is filled with people who choose to be evil, but I can't control them. All I can do is trust our crew, and trust that we're better prepared in the future.

"Do you really think this is gonna work?"

I nod my head seriously as I continue to walk. I've been doing everything I can think of to help this baby get *out* of me. Spicy blood, orgasms, nipple stimulation-- though that last one apparently isn't going to work because it's Jeff's nipples I've mostly been playing with. In my defense, see point number two.

"It's gonna work. This baby is coming today. I can just feel it."

Ronny hums. "If you say so."

"I do. Trust me." Being a vampire means I don't really sweat, but walking up and down this street over and over is leaving all my limbs tired. My right leg is up on the curb while my left foot is on the street. I'd read online this was a great way to get things going and at this point, I'm willing to try anything.

"I thought you were enjoying being pregnant."

"I was. But now I'm over it. I'm tired and sore and *huge*. I want this baby *out* of me so Jeff can carry them and give me a break."

Ronny snorts in amusement, walking right next to me and making sure I'm okay. Cooper sits in front of my apartment, a beer resting next to him and a book in his lap. I know the other guys are just upstairs in my apartment, waiting for me to come inside. Joke's on them, I'm not going up there until it's time. I will out-stubborn this child.

I look up at my window, finding Jeff there watching us. I give him a giant wave before going back to walking.

I turn around and start walking in the opposite direction, switching which foot is up on the curb. I see someone walking towards me and I put my hands in the front of my hoodie, pulling it forward to help hide my stomach as best as I can. Ronny's body language changes, being more on alert. My stomach warms, knowing all of these guys love and care about me and the baby. I love them all too.

"Oh. Hi Star!"

The woman walking towards me is a short, older woman that Dakota introduced me to. He promised that she was an amazing midwife and would help take care of me during my pregnancy. True to his words, she's been wonderful. I recognize her a distance away because of her stark white hair that has the littlest streak of dark purple in it.

"Hello," she calls out, a wide smile gracing her lips as she walks over to us. Ronny relaxes beside me, recognizing who this is. "It seems I'm a little early."

"What do you mean?" Ronny asks just before I freeze.

"Fuck," I blurt out, looking down and watching as wetness spread across my pants.

"Never mind. I'm right on time."

Ronny and Star quickly usher me upstairs to my apartment. Jeff quickly stands up, rushing over to me. "Did you pee yourself?"

"No," I say right away, narrowing my eyes at him. "My water broke! I wouldn't pee myself, Jeff!"

"I hear that's normal," Martin says with a chuckle. "Nothing to be ashamed of, Axel."

"Fuck you, Martin."

Pain lances through my middle, making me pause and breathe through it. Jeff is by my side right away, holding onto me. I tuck my face against his chest, letting his scent soothe some of the pain away. Knowing my mate is here with me, knowing that Star is here to help puts some of my worries to rest. I'm okay. I can do this with them by my side.

Star and Jeff take me to my bedroom. Jeff carefully helps me out of my wet clothes as Star strips my bed, getting everything ready. My chest warms, realizing just how well cared for I am. I used to be alone and now I'm surrounded by people who love me. Lady Fate has blessed me beyond what I knew to wish for.

"How did you know I would need you?"

Star raises her brow, giving me a small smile. Something about this woman makes me feel small, like she's all knowing. Yet, I feel completely safe in her presence.

"Call it intuition," she finally says, "or maybe Dakota mentioned you were ready to use any means necessary to get this baby out."

Another cramp goes through my middle, making my stomach tense up. I grit my teeth until it's over. "I've gotten my wish," I say with a long sigh.

Jeff kisses the side of my head. "You've got this, baby. You're so strong and our baby is almost here."

I tug Jeff into our bed, putting him against the headboard. Then I arrange myself so I'm up on my knees, holding onto his shoulders in front of me. I bury my face against his throat, letting his scent ground me as I experience my contractions. He keeps me grounded, keeps me relaxed.

"You're doing amazing," Star tells me, guiding me through labor, helping me read the instincts of getting this baby out of me.

I'm not sure how long we sit there before I feel a pressure below my waist. "Okay," I murmur, my brows wrinkled, "I think it's time."

"Take a deep breath and bare down," Star tells me.

I bite Jeff's shoulder and he sucks in a sharp breath. His arms go around my back, holding me as I push. "You can do this. Just a little more, baby."

I can feel the moment our baby slides free and my eyes prickle with emotion. If I was able to cry I know I would be shedding tears right now. Relief so deep it threatens to be my undoing washes over me and I let out a broken noise. I pull away from Jeff's shoulder to look at him, the emotions I'm feeling mirror in his eyes.

"You did it," he tells me proudly. "You fucking did it, Axel. You've given me *everything*."

Jeff helps me to rearrange and Star hands me my baby. She is *beautiful*. She has dark hair just like Jeff and has my nose. I love her so much.

Star hands me a bottle and I didn't even realize she had one ready. I bring it to my baby's lips, watching as she sucks greedily straight away.

"It's jarring," Jeff says softly, "seeing her drink from a blood bottle."

I snort. "She's a vampire, what else would she drink."

"No, no. It makes sense. Just kinda weird to see still," he

says, nuzzling against the side of my head. Newborns don't need much so our baby is quickly full. I pull the bottle away, bringing her up against my chest.

"Have you thought of her name?"

"Lily," I tell Star with a wide smile.

"That's beautiful. Very fitting."

"Thank you," Jeff says softly. He kisses my head. I look into his eyes, finding nothing but unabashed love there.

"Here," I whisper, handing Jeff his daughter for the first time. The way he holds her with such tender care fills me with warmth. I am so lucky that Lady Fate saw this man fit to be my mate. He's everything I need in my life. I give him stability and he gives me adventure. We fit.

"I love you so much," Jeff tells me. "Thank you so much, Axel."

"You have nothing to thank me for. I'm just doing my best to be the best mate I can be."

"You're that and so much more."

When our lips meet, everything else falls away until it's just me and my true mate sharing a tender moment. And in the next moment, Star is clearing her throat. If I was capable of blushing I know I would be bright red right now.

She gives the two of us a tender smile, like a mother gives her children. I'm not sure I could be happier than I am right now. That is, until the rest of the crew come in here to meet Lily.

EPILOGUE
JEFF

I CARRY Lily in my hands, cradling her tiny head in the palm of my hand. She's perfect, absolutely perfect. The love I have for Axel is overwhelming, it's like a storm blowing me away. But the love I have for Lily is different. It's warm, wiggling its way into the center of my chest.

Star tucks the blankets around Axel, making sure he's comfortable before turning towards me. "Shall I let the others in? They're practically radiating with excited tension from the other room."

I snort, smiling so wide that my cheeks hurt. "Yeah, let them in. Thank you."

"You're welcome," Star says, stopping to squeeze my shoulder. "You've done well. Protecting, bringing these people together, being a mate. You should be proud of yourself, Jeff." Her eyes sparkle with something I can't quite name but there's something about this woman that draws me in. I believe her words and they warm me all over. "Consider yourself redeemed. Let yourself live now, okay?"

I swallow thickly, nodding my head. "I'll do my best."

"That's all I ask," she murmurs before turning and leaving the room.

I step over to the bed, sitting beside Axel's hip and he runs his hand down my spine. "Star is absolutely right, I hope you know that."

"It's starting to sink in," I confess softly.

Before I can say more, the guys are walking into the room. "Oh my gods," Cooper says, stepping over to me and looking down at Lily with giant eyes. "She's so perfect."

"I couldn't agree more," Axel says with a wide smile. Cooper looks at us with wide, longing eyes and my chest clenches for him. He'll get this. They all will. I can just feel it.

"Everyone," I say, looking over at Martin, Cooper, and Carlos, "meet the newest member of our crew. This is Lily."

"She's beautiful," Carlos tells us.

"Where's Ronny?" Axel asks, looking around worriedly.

"He'll be right here," Martin says, "he stepped outside for a moment."

"He mentioned he might have found our next case," Cooper says as he reaches down, petting over Lily's head gently. "But only if you guys feel like moving. We understand if you need a break after all this."

Axel speaks up before I can. "I'm ready for a change and I'm sure Lily will be fine traveling. She'll probably just sleep all the way there."

"Can I hold her?"

I'm surprised by the question but my chest warms as I carefully had Lily over to Martin. He's built like a brick wall and yet, holds my daughter so carefully. It's absolutely precious and I don't miss how the look of longing on Cooper's face intensifies as he watches.

Axel leans his head against me as we watch our family meet Lily. I'm overwhelmed with emotion at the sight of everyone loving on my daughter. This is everything I never knew I needed.

Eventually, Ronny joins us, holding his hoodie in his hands.

"Ronny, come meet Lily," Martin says with a wide smile but we all freeze when we hear the tiniest meow.

"I umm, I might have found a new friend," Ronny says sheepishly.

Carlos runs over and Ronny takes a step back, protecting the bundle in his arms. That's interesting. "Sorry, I just wanted to see."

"That's okay. Just be careful, they're hurt."

Carlos nods his head before gently pulling Ronny's sweater back. In his arms are two cats, one considerably smaller than the other. "Ronny, they're--"

"Hurt. I know. I found them outside and I couldn't just let them go. So I grabbed them. I'll take good care of them," Ronny says, gently touching the adult cat's head. The cat leans into his touch, letting out the tiniest little meow.

"Are you sure you wanna take them on the road with us, Ronny? I heard you found us a new job," I say carefully.

He nods his head and I can tell he's already determined. "I can take care of them, no worries, bossman."

"Alright," I say, "then I think our plans are set." I turn towards Axel. "Do you think you're up for a road trip tomorrow?"

Axel nuzzles my shoulder. "I'll rest for the night and be good to go in the morning."

With our plans on the book, I lean back in our bed and watch as our daughter gets passed around. Without a doubt I know this entire crew will do everything they can to watch over her and make sure she grows up strong and taken care of. I kiss the side of Axel's head, saying another silent prayer up to Lady Fate, thanking her for this family and adding an extra special note, asking that she watches over my crew the same way she's watched over me.

I can't wait to see what our next chapter will be but already I know it's going to be good.

THE END

Want a FREE prequel story for the Collection of Hunters series? Grab **Between Hunts** now and get to know the rest of the hunters.

Looking for more of the hunters? Check out *Hunting for Love* as Ronny finds love in the form of a hurt cat shifter.

If you want to get the latest news from Toby, sign up for **Toby's Newsletter**! He'll keep you informed on new releases, sales, and any exciting news you'll wanna be in the know for.

Plus, you can join **Toby's Patreon** for exclusive content, cover reveals, teasers, and a brand new Patron chosen story!

MORE FROM TOBY WISE

A Collection of Hunters

Between Hunts (Prequel)

Hunting for Redemption

Hunting for Love

A Collection of Strays

Before Fate (Prequel)

Ageless Fate

Touching Fate

Fate's Perfect Timing

Trusting Fate

Submitting to Fate

Bite Sized Fate (Short Story)

Fate's Final Chapter

A Collection of Strays: The Boxset

Studio C

Watching Me

Feral for You

Choosing Me

True For You

ABOUT THE AUTHOR

Toby Wise is a stay at home parent who hails from a tiny town in Wisconsin. Contrary to popular Wisconsin stereotypes, he's not a cheese-head who enjoys beer but rather an introvert who spends all his time on the internet, drinking coffee, spending time with his kid, and cooing about his adorable cat, Pikachu.

In April of 2019, A Collection of Strays was born after the world of fanfiction drew him back into his love of writing. Now he's writing all things omegaverse as long as it includes silly moments and found family.

Facebook Group: Toby's Wiseasses
Toby's Patreon ← Join for exclusive content, early teasers, and ARC's of future books
Sign up for my Newsletter Here ← Stay up to date on Toby's newest releases
Toby's Website ← Find all Toby's books, announcements and freebies in one place.

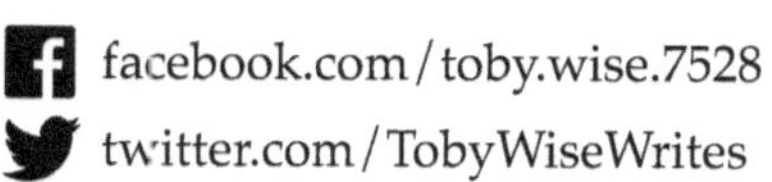

www.ingramcontent.com/pod-product-compliance
Lightning Source LLC
Chambersburg PA
CBHW020733160726

47993CB00006B/2426